# Stranded in Love

*Amber —*

*Happy Reading!*

*Victoria*

# VICTORIA
# GRANT

Tellwell Talent
www.tellwell.ca

ISBN
978-1-77370-099-1 (Hardcover)
978-1-77370-100-4 (Paperback)
978-1-77370-098-4 (eBook)

## DEDICATION

*For Larry,*

my love,

my light,

my everything

# Chapter 1

"I don't believe this! Not again! Not *tonight!*"

Laney Calderone pounded her gloved hands on the steering wheel and gazed around hopelessly. Why couldn't she be taking a midnight dip in the warm, inviting waters off Tahiti, or dancing the night away at that fun little club in Belize City, or enjoying an après ski party with friends in St. Moritz? But, no, karma truly hated her, because she was stuck in a deserted downtown Toronto parking lot in the freezing cold, with dollops of snowflakes rapidly descending upon her brand new but disabled car. And that was the cherry on the top of a really bad day.

She shivered and turned the key once more hoping her fairy godmother, if indeed she had one, had decided to magically repair the defective part. But the car gave a painful whirr and shuddered to its ultimate end.

"So much for fairy godmothers. I never believed in fairy tales, anyway," Laney complained miserably to the cold, empty darkness surrounding her. "And so the worst day of my life continues."

Laney, the twenty-four-year-old only daughter and youngest sibling in Toronto's wealthy and powerful Calderone family, was a Vice President at Calderone Industries, the family business and leading telecommunications company in Canada. And she had been, until this evening, engaged to be married to Mr. Ramone DeSantis, the son of the owner of one of CI's largest competitors. Her mother had decided in order for CI to buy out the DeSantis Group, which CI liked to do with all their competitors, large and small, it would be easier if Laney were married to the owner's son. Laney didn't love Ramone; she never did. However, her mother, being a formidable force, was not a lady you argued with unless you did it just for the practice, because you were going to lose, guaranteed. And Laney's engagement was proof of that. She'd lost count of how many times she and her mother had argued about this.

And, as Laney discovered earlier in the day, she was not only a VP in the family business, she was also in the family way. How the heck had she gotten pregnant? Okay, stupid question, but she'd had sex with Ramone less than a dozen times, and they'd always used a condom! Unbelievable!

She'd chosen to tell Ramone about her pregnancy at their dinner tonight, and had figured because they'd be married in three months anyway, it wasn't that big a deal, was it? It was. Ramone had gone ballistic, screaming at Laney that he never wanted kids and blaming her entirely for this pregnancy. He had stormed out of the restaurant, but not before he'd called off their engagement and taken the ring back. Actually, Laney had thrown the ring at him when her patience and manners had reached their limit, but the end result was the same — no February wedding and a baby on the way.

The engagement being called off was not at all distressing for Laney, she was quite relieved about that. The pregnancy, however, was a shocker. How was she ever going to explain this to her family, especially her ultra conservative and conventional thinking mother? Genevieve Calderone would not react well to either event, and Laney didn't even want to think about the catastrophe which would ensue once her mother found out. But right now, her pregnancy, her broken engagement, and her mother's reactions to them would all have to wait. She had to get home. But how?

She grabbed her cell phone out of her purse then tossed it onto the passenger seat with mounting frustration when she realized she'd forgotten to recharge it that morning. It was lifeless.

"No help there. Okay, Plan B." Laney sighed as she pulled on her beret and tightened the scarf around her neck. She had no idea what Plan B was, though she knew she'd freeze to death if she didn't do something. Climbing out of the flame red MG, the blinding snow and wind momentarily knocked the breath from her. Looking up, she noticed the street lights casting barely a shadow through the heavily falling flakes.

Laney slammed the door shut then lifted the hood. Now, she thought, what exactly is it I'm supposed to be looking for? Her eyes roamed the assorted engine circuitry wishing she could see a flashing neon sign with the words *Push this Button to Restart Engine*.

No such luck. The heavy, wet snow covered the engine and she shivered again trying to brace herself against the powerful squalls.

"Need any help?" a deep voice penetrated the howling wind.

Laney heaved another sigh as she looked up and saw someone approaching. "No, of course not!" she snapped, in no mood for stupid questions. "I often come out here late at night during raging blizzards to study the complexities of my car engine! Would you like to join me? Perhaps later we could pop into the coffee shop down the street for a latté and scone, just to finish the evening off right."

A low chuckle escaped the stranger's lips. "All right, as you seem to have the situation under control, I'll leave you to it. Goodnight."

"Wait —" Through the swirls of snow Laney was now very much aware of the man approaching. Her eyes took in his massive shoulders hidden beneath a black leather jacket, and as he got closer, her gaze wandered higher taking in the full lips creased in a smile, a finely chiselled nose and steel grey eyes that seemed to be twinkling, then thick, dark curls which refused to be flattened by the huge, wet flakes.

"Sorry...this hasn't been a great day for me and now *this!* Not my idea of fun." She stamped her feet in a futile effort to thaw her toes.

His smile widened. "What's the trouble?"

Was he completely dense? "If I knew that, would I be standing here freezing to death apologizing to a total stranger?"

Her stinging reply didn't seem to bother him as his laugh broke the snowy silence. "Now, now," he scolded. "Let's start again. I'm Tyler Hammond. And you are?"

"Cold, tired, hungry, and fed up." She didn't bother adding pregnant, it was none of his business.

He raised an amused eyebrow. "Charming."

Laney treated him to her most withering glare, then checked her watch. "Look, it's getting late and I'd like to get home. Can you help me or not?"

"I'll call you Jane. That'll make this a little easier."

"Jane? *Jane?* I don't think so! I'm Alaina Calderone. Call me Laney."

"Hello Laney. It's almost a pleasure to meet you." He grinned.

She shivered once more as Tyler turned his attention to her car. "Let's have a look. Any idea why she won't start?"

"How should I know?" Laney rapidly came to the conclusion that Tyler Hammond was a complete moron.

"It *is* your car. I thought you might know something about it."

She stared at him. "Is there a new law that states Ontario citizens must be licensed mechanics to own and operate a motor vehicle in this province?"

"It would help," he said dryly.

"Well, unfortunately, I left my mechanic's handy roadside repair manual at home tonight."

"Too bad. You could certainly use it now." He leaned over and examined a few of the engine parts. "Is the key in the ignition?"

When she nodded, he climbed behind the wheel. Laney heard the painful whirr again and sighed heavily, realizing to her disappointment that Tyler Hammond was no mechanic. Still, her hopes weren't high.

He climbed out of the car and smiled far too cheerfully for her liking. "Nope, she won't start."

"Brilliant deduction! Any other extraordinary insights you'd like to share with me, Sherlock?"

"You're not earning many points for Miss Congeniality, you know." He tried unsuccessfully to hide a smirk.

"I beg your pardon?"

"Never mind. Where do you live?"

*"What?"* Laney stopped stamping her feet, it wasn't helping anyway; her toes were frozen. She stared at him.

Tyler took a deep breath. "It's a simple question, Miss Calderone. Where do you live? I'll take you home."

"I hardly know you!"

The muscles in his neck tensed and his brow knotted. "Don't flatter yourself. I was only trying to help."

"How do I know that? You're a complete stranger to me."

"Look, your car isn't going anywhere tonight, is it?" his voice bristled. "So I'm offering you a ride home. If you have a cell phone, you could call someone to come for you, but I think you're smart enough to have thought of that by now, which tells me either you couldn't reach anyone, or whoever you did call isn't going to brave this storm, am I right?"

"My cell battery is dead. Can I use yours?"

"My cell is in a hundred pieces a block and a half from here, so it's not much good to either of us." Tyler squinted as the heavy flakes continued to fall. He needed to get home, have a stiff drink, and put his lousy day behind him, but it looked like Miss Congeniality was going to delay those plans. "I would suggest you review your options quickly, the storm looks like it's getting worse. I am offering to drive you home or you can stay here and freeze to death. Entirely your choice."

Laney's scalp prickled as a flood of questions and concerns battled in her head for answers. Who was this guy? Where had he been to show up now and offer assistance? Would he really take her home? Did he look like a mass- murderer, whatever they looked like? Could she trust this Poster Boy for TDH's? Because now she'd taken a good long look at him, he was indeed Tall, Dark, Handsome, and more.

"I'm waiting."

"I'm thinking." Laney had to admit she had no other way of getting home. She was going to have to trust this TDH/Good Samaritan. "Okay, I'll get my things."

Tyler stood motionless, a giant monolith serenely oblivious to the winter storm raging around him. Laney quickly grabbed her purse and keys.

"Let's go, my car's in the next lot." Tyler offered his arm to help Laney fight the brutal wind, but she refused it. They made their way down the street, where Laney could see a single car, cold and still, cloaked in a thick mantle of snow.

"What if your car won't start?" she asked, quickening her strides to keep up with him.

He threw her a wicked grin. "We'll both freeze our asses off, won't we?"

They approached the sleek, black BMW and Tyler unlocked the passenger door and held it open while Laney climbed in. After swiftly clearing the snow from the windows, he slid his imposing form in beside her. The car roared to life on the first try. Laney concentrated intently on the falling flakes in front of her, ignoring the smiling face that had turned her way.

After they'd been travelling for a few minutes, Tyler asked Laney where she lived.

"Forest Hill," she replied.

"Why didn't you tell me this five minutes ago? Now I have to double back to get onto the highway," he said, more than slightly annoyed.

Laney shrugged. "You should've asked sooner."

Tyler slammed on the brakes with a sudden savagery, the car swerving perilously on the icy road. The force bounced Laney roughly against the door, and as the car came to a stop he glared at her. "Do you want to walk home?" he threatened.

She straightened in her seat, then slowly turned to him. "That's not very nice. You did offer to take me home."

Tyler sighed. "God, I feel sorry for your husband."

"I'm not married."

"I'm not surprised."

"What does *that* mean?"

Tyler silently manoeuvred the car carefully onto the road and turned the windshield wipers on faster to combat the rapid accumulation of snow. When he spoke, his tone was harsh.

"All I've done is offer my assistance to you, Miss Calderone, and all I've gotten from you in return is complaints and criticism. No man could put up with that for very long."

"Well, forgive me if I'm not kissing your ass to thank you for your gesture of kindness, Mr. Hammond. I've just experienced the worst day of my life and it's *all* because of a man."

A frosty and uncomfortable silence followed as Laney replayed the entire day's and evening's events in her mind. Then her slender body began trembling and try as she might she couldn't stop the flow of tears. Her hands covered her face as the sobs shook her petite frame, and Tyler, without taking his eyes off the road, stuffed his handkerchief into her hands. Minutes later when the tears subsided, she took a deep breath.

"Yes...I'm okay...thanks for...asking," she delivered sarcastically between hiccups.

"I've never known anyone who couldn't survive a few tears." There wasn't a trace of emotion in his voice.

"You heartless...beast!"

"Let's get one thing straight right now. I'm a stranger to you. You don't know me. I don't know you. I'm simply doing you a favour. That's it. That's all. I've had quite a lousy day too, Miss Calderone, and this isn't my idea of a joy ride. Now sit back and be quiet. These roads are as icy as hell and it's not making the drive any easier with you whining in my ear."

Laney's eyes widened as he spoke. *"Whining in your ear?!* How...*dare* you —"

"Be quiet!" Tyler growled. "Or I'll shut you up for good."

Laney heaved a lengthy sigh and sat very still. Her lips tightened as they always did when she was fuming, however, she knew to say anything now would be asking for more nasty comments, or worse, from her Good Samaritan.

Who was this moody stranger? Whoever he was, Laney was certain his day had not been nearly as bad as hers. She turned to study his face which was mostly hidden in the shadows. She noticed his steel grey eyes intensely focused on the road ahead, his thick, dark eyebrows furrowed in concentration. His cheeks looked soft and smooth, no stubble to interfere with the strong line of his jaw. His thick dark brown curls framed his face and rested gently on his collar. But it was his lips that made Laney curious about his day. They tightened when they passed under the street lights, yet when the shadows returned, they seemed to crease into a grin. A tiny, almost imperceptible grin, but a grin nonetheless. Exactly what was going through his mind? And how lousy could his day have been if his thoughts made him smile?

Tyler quickly glanced her way. "See something you like?"

Laney's eyes darted back to the road. "Just drive."

The man was probably an escaped lunatic who liked to trap unsuspecting women in his car and shout at them, she thought, as her hand fumbled in the dark to find the door latch in case she needed to make a quick escape. Locked. Laney sighed. Sure it was. Karma strikes again. Oh well, Plan C wasn't going to happen. Can't wait to see what Plan D has in store for me.

As they neared the on-ramp to the highway, a couple of police cars blocked the way, all lights flashing, and an officer dressed in a heavy parka and gloves waved them over to the shoulder.

"Now what?" Tyler muttered, lowering his window. "What's the problem, officer?"

The policeman leaned in through the window to make himself heard above the gusts of wind whipping around him. "There's been a bad accident half a mile down the highway, sir. We've had to close this section. It'll probably be closed all night." He looked up, straining to see as the flakes fell into his eyes.

"Right. So, what's my best route to Forest Hill?" Tyler asked.

The officer thought for a moment. "You'll have to go around the north end of the city, and without the benefit of the highway, it's going to take quite a while in this weather."

"How long, would you say?"

"Oh, at least an hour to get there, maybe closer to two or more if the snow keeps falling like this."

Tyler nodded. "An hour or two. Or more. Okay, thank you officer. Goodnight."

"Goodnight sir. Goodnight ma'am. Drive safely."

Tyler closed the window and slowly turned the car around. Laney noticed his gloved hands were tightly clenching the steering wheel and she wondered if she should apologize for causing so much trouble, then decided against it. God knows what he would do if she spoke again. Besides, he hadn't really wanted to help her. She didn't need him to spell it out for her again. He had been in the wrong place at the wrong time, a situation Laney was very familiar with.

They travelled in uneasy silence again for a few minutes until Laney realized they were not heading north. "Where are you going?"

Tyler concentrated on the road. "My place."

"*What!?*"

"You heard me. I'm not driving for two hours or more in this insufferable stuff so you can sleep in your cozy little bed. We'll be at my place in twenty minutes, unless a major disaster occurs. You can call a cab from there."

# Chapter 2

Twenty-five minutes later, Tyler smoothly glided the BMW into the long driveway of one of Toronto's finest luxury condominium high-rises. Laney couldn't hide her surprise. She could tell by his clothes and his car that he wasn't a vagabond, but she hadn't expected this.

"You live *here*?"

"I know it's a far cry from Forest Hill, Miss Calderone, so humour me, would you?"

A tiny smile creased her lips.

"Ah, so you do know how to smile. I'd been wondering." He grinned and handed his keys to the valet. They exchanged a few comments about the snowfall as Tyler offered his hand to help Laney out of the car. She followed him to the main doors.

Once inside, Laney was surrounded by the elegance of the entrance foyer. Stylish yet traditional furniture rested on the highly polished hardwood floor beneath her boots. Fresh flowers in crystal vases sat on every table top, beautiful artwork adorned the walls, and the entire area conveyed a graceful charm Laney found soothing and comforting. And it was warm.

"Coming?" Tyler waited for her beside the bank of elevators.

"Isn't there a telephone here I could use?" Her eyes scanned the foyer again.

"No. We don't like loiterers. You'll have to come up with me."

Laney stared at him, a thousand protests coming to mind. "I'd rather not. Perhaps you could call a cab for me and I'll wait here." She sneezed.

"No, you're coming with me. Besides, it'll give you a chance to warm up. Don't worry, Miss Calderone, I won't take advantage of you in any way." There seemed to be a hint of compassion in his voice, yet the second it came through, his condescending tone shot it down.

Okay, Plan D not going well, Laney mused, don't even want to think about Plan E, although she knew not many damsels in distress ever got to Plan E. At least not in any movie she'd ever seen. This should be interesting. She joined him in the elevator.

As they rode to the fourteenth floor, Tyler finally took a long look at Laney's reflection in the mirrored elevator walls while she avoided eye contact and concentrated on the buttons. Smooth, clear skin, thick golden blonde hair that cascaded halfway down her back, a pert little nose and warm, dark brown eyes. Her blue jeans were tucked into black leather high heel boots, and her black leather gloves, beret, and scarf accented her white ski jacket.

The elevator doors finally opened and Laney followed Tyler down the long hallway to the last door. When his key clicked into the lock, she stepped tentatively through the door, and when he flicked on the lights she took in her surroundings. Beyond the small entrance hallway was a huge living-dining area with a floor to ceiling gas fireplace in the centre. Comfy white furniture sat scattered throughout with red and black accent pieces here and there, and winter white carpeting and black hardwood floors completed the dramatic effect.

Tyler tossed his jacket onto a chair and headed for the black lacquered bar in the corner. "Drink?" he offered.

"Earl Grey tea, please, with honey and lemon." Laney shivered as she pulled off her boots, then slowly took off her beret and gloves and unravelled the scarf from her neck.

Watching her every move, Tyler said, "it's no surprise you're shivering. How can you stay warm in this weather in a *leather scarf?!*"

She ignored his comment. "What are you drinking?"

"It's not tea."

"So I gathered. Can I have tea, or is it your maid's night off?"

"You could have, although I'm sure by the time I went to all the trouble of making it, your cab would be here." He smiled, saluting her with his glass, then downed the amber liquid.

"Fine. Where's your phone?"

"In there." He pointed to a set of white French doors to her right that Laney quickly passed through. She shut the doors behind her, then turned to look at the biggest bed she had ever seen. It stood at the far end of a rectangular-shaped room decorated in the same colours as the living room. A white furry blanket covered the bed, red and black pillows in assorted geometric shapes had been carelessly tossed on top of it. The huge floor to ceiling window was behind the bed, and with the black blinds open, provided a magnificent view of the snowstorm and the white city below.

Moving towards the window, Laney spotted the red telephone on the bedside table. She reached into her purse for her cell phone, remembered she had no power to access her contact list, and tossed it back into her purse, cursing. She sat on the edge of the bed and dialled 411 for directory assistance. After a dozen rings she hung up. "Damn it!"

"Problem?" Without her being aware of it, Tyler had come into the room and stood with his back against the door cradling another drink.

"Do you have a phone book? Seems all the directory assistants have gone home for the evening."

"Bottom shelf in the night stand."

Laney reached for it and pulled the heavy book out of its hiding place. Impatiently she flipped through it, aware of him watching her every move. It unnerved her that he was staring at her. Hadn't he ever seen a person look up a phone number before? Didn't he have anything better to do? Sliding into the path of an oncoming bus came to mind. She finally found the taxi cab section and tried the first number.

"Yes, hello. I'd like a cab right away, please. *None* available? Then, I'll wait...oh, I see...at least three hours, maybe longer. Forget it."

Tyler continued to watch her as she dialled the next number.

"I'd like a taxi...yes, I know there's a blizzard out there...I have to get home!...No, you don't understand... No, it's... Oh, never mind!" Laney slammed the phone down as Tyler came closer. She felt the bed tilt slightly as he sat down. She quickly punched in another number. After a few minutes with no response, she hung up.

"I don't believe this! You'd think Toronto had never experienced a snowstorm before! Pathetic cabbies! The snivelling cowards are too scared to drive in this weather!"

"Poor little Laney."

She glared at him. His drink was apparently a double, like the one before it. "Take me home," she demanded. "Now."

Tyler laughed. "You must be joking. I'm not leaving here again tonight."

"Yes, you are. You're taking me home."

"I'm in no fit state to take you anywhere."

Laney shot off the bed, her stomach plummeting to the floor as a subtle yet persistent sense of foreboding began to crawl into every nerve ending. She didn't want or need to analyze it, she just knew she had to get out of there, now.

"You did that on purpose, didn't you? First, you won't drive a little bit out of your way to take me home, then you make me come up here against my better judgement, then you start drinking so you *can't* drive me home! How convenient! The next thing I know, you'll have your filthy paws all over me!"

Tyler stood up directly in front of her, his eyes darkening, his fingers choking the glass he was holding. He drained the last of the scotch, then, without warning, hurled the empty glass against the white marble fireplace reposing stately in the centre of the wall. Laney flinched as the glass shattered and a million tiny shards scattered across the floor.

"Despite what you might think," he spat, "I am not enjoying spending this time with you, Miss Calderone. In fact, I'm sincerely regretting offering you my assistance. Believe me when I say that the very *last* thing I want to do is toss you onto my bed and make wild, passionate love to you." His metallic grey eyes fired into silver sparks and the muscles strained in his neck. His voice became a whisper. "Although if I did, I would no doubt teach you a thing or two, I'm sure."

Even with her body's quaking that nearly sent her collapsing onto the bed, Laney laughed out loud. "You really think you're quite *something*, don't you, Mr. Hammond?" She moved a step closer to him, a terrifying yet tempting lure holding her captive.

"And *you* think you know everything, don't you, Miss Calderone? Like all the ways to please a man, perhaps?" He took a step forward.

"I know most men aren't worth the effort." Laney's cheeks blazed as she moved to within inches of his face.

"Possibly, but I'm sure I could show you a few interesting moves to add to your repertoire."

Laney's hands went to her hips, her quaking now powerful enough to register on every worldwide Richter scale. "Oh, you think so, do you?" She stood defiantly.

"I do." His hand caught hers and pulled her roughly to him, then fiercely covered her mouth with his. Tyler's hands clutched her shoulders, mercilessly trapping her against him. He crushed her slight contours against his broad chest, and Laney was rooted to the floor. She felt the raw hunger in his rough kiss, tasted the alcohol on his warm lips, all the while an unfamiliar dizziness swept through her. She couldn't move even if she wanted to, and, in a sudden flash of enlightenment, she very clearly understood the meaning of the word *ravish*.

Moments later he pushed her away. "Seems I was right. You *do* have a lot to learn about pleasing a man."

Laney sharply slapped his face. "You despicable bastard!" She took a step back and furiously wiped her hand across her mouth trying to rid her lips of the lingering heat. "Keep your filthy hands off me!"

"I rather think you enjoyed it; however, the feeling wasn't mutual."

"Don't flatter yourself, Mr. Hammond! I'm not one of those cheap trollops you no doubt bring here on a regular basis who are impressed with your fast car, your fast talk, and your fast hands!" She grabbed her purse off the bed, her stomach churning. "But you're not impressing *me*! Now take me home!"

Tyler's smile was filled with contempt. "I could've sworn I just finished telling you I'm on the way to drowning out my miserable day. I'm in no condition to drive."

"You don't have a monopoly on miserable days, Mr. Hammond. Where are your keys? I'll drive your car home and return it tomorrow." Laney's eyes searched the room.

"Don't be a fool. You did see me give them to the valet, didn't you?"

"Yes, but you must have a spare set around here somewhere."

"No, I don't. You'll have to stay here tonight."

"Don't make me laugh! Stay here? With *you*?!" she scoffed.

"Are you a coward as well as a spoilt little brat?"

She saw the challenge in his eyes and headed for the door. "I've taken as much as I'm going to take from you, Mr. Hammond! You've proven to me yet again that all men are assholes!" she stormed out of the bedroom and slammed the door behind her.

Laney swiftly pulled on her boots, grabbed her coat, and opened the door. But reality, with a side order of karma, stopped her cold—she was stuck. No car, no cell phone, not a taxi to be had, a relentless snowstorm, and nowhere near home. Her shoulders sank as she turned to find Tyler standing a few feet away.

"Changed your mind so soon? You disappoint me, Laney," he chided. "Where's all your Calderone determination? Aren't you going to go outside to brave the elements for at least a few minutes before coming to your senses and turning back? That would certainly earn you an A for effort." He strolled to the bar and poured himself another drink.

Laney stood silent and motionless in the entry hall, torn between leaving, crying, and wanting to punch him in that superb yet spiteful mouth of his. She waited for him to extend the invitation to stay again, then, she thought, I'll tell him a thing or two! She watched as he got comfortable, preoccupied with his own thoughts, entirely oblivious to her presence.

Minutes later, when he had still not spoken a word, Laney turned to go. To hell with him, she thought. I'm not a complete idiot. There must be a way to get home even if I die trying!

"Decided not to stay, then?" Tyler's voice boomed in the quiet room. "Perhaps you do have more spunk than I originally gave you credit for. Good luck in trying to get home. You do have an alternative, remember."

"Is that your idea of an invitation?"

"Take it as you like. You don't need me to list your options."

"How true. I don't need you for anything."

"Seriously? I don't believe you'd be doing too well at this moment if I hadn't passed by that parking lot when I did."

Laney's eyes widened. "Are you saying you *saved my life*? What *arrogance*!"

Tyler was beside her in an instant. "It's time you realized, Miss Calderone, that no one is an island. We all need help now and again, even if we're too stupid or too stubborn to admit it!" He lowered his voice. "It's also time you learned not all men are assholes intent on using and abusing women."

"You have *no* right to say those things to me." Her voice faltered, emotion welling up again, tears ready to fall. "You have no idea what's happened to me today..."

They stood staring at each other for what seemed an eternity, then Tyler let out a long agonizing breath, his hostility gradually dissolving with it, and he reached for her hand and gently squeezed it.

"I'm sorry, Laney. You're right, I don't know what you've been through today and it's none of my business. But I can't let you walk out of here in this weather with no way of getting home. Please stay." His voice was soft, his touch gentle, his thumb rubbing delicate circles on the top of her hand. "You have nowhere else to go and this snow isn't going to stop for a while. I promise I'll take you home tomorrow."

"I can't stay." Hot tears burned Laney's eyes, nausea rumbled through her belly.

"Please," he whispered.

Laney was torn. She wanted to shout and scream at him because of how he'd treated her, and because of the difficult situation she found herself in. But she knew she had no way out. Not tonight. Dropping her things, she allowed him to take her back into the living room.

He sat her in front of the fire, kneeled down beside her and pulled off her boots. He turned up the fire so the flames shot high into the air. Laney shivered.

"Still cold?" he smiled. "It's that thin little sweater. I'll get you one of mine to put on, it'll help you warm up faster." He disappeared into the bedroom and Laney put her head back and closed her eyes. Her hands rested on her stomach; her nausea persisted.

Tyler returned with a pair of his bedroom slippers, a thick fisherman's knit sweater, and a black furry afghan. Silently, he pulled her off the sofa and helped her put his sweater on over the top of hers, then he wrapped the blanket snugly around her. Once she sat down again, he kneeled in front of her and pressed the warm slippers onto her feet. They were huge, but she welcomed the warmth.

"Thank you."

"You're welcome. Would you like that cup of tea now?" he smiled.

"Yes, please." She nodded. "Why are you suddenly being so nice to me? A few minutes ago, you looked like you wanted to choke the life out of me."

He stood up, his eyes twinkling. "I think I like you, Laney. You're different from the 'trollops'." He winked.

She cringed. "Sorry about that."

"Laney, look, I know we're not friends, but it doesn't mean we have to be enemies, right? Why don't we try to get along? Okay?"

"Okay."

"Shall we start again then, on the right foot this time?"

"Yes, I'd like that." She smiled.

"You should smile more often, Laney. You're quite beautiful when you do."

There was something in those silver pools he called eyes, but before Laney could determine exactly what emotion she'd witnessed, Tyler walked away to another wall where he touched a button and light flooded into a large kitchen. He climbed three steps, and Laney watched him prepare the tea in a kitchen decorated like the rest of his home, with a black and white parquet floor and red and black accessories.

"Are you hungry?" he asked her. "I didn't have any dinner tonight. I lost my appetite right before it was served. Have you eaten?"

"No, actually, I haven't."

Minutes later, Tyler handed her a mug of hot tea. "Would you like something stronger? A scotch or brandy, perhaps?"

She wrapped her hands around the mug. "This is fine, thank you." Again, she shivered uncontrollably.

"You're not warming up. Perhaps you've caught a chill."

"I'll be okay." She sipped the hot liquid, letting it slide down her raw throat.

"Why don't you have a hot bath?" Tyler suggested. "And I'll make us dinner while you're soaking."

"No, I don't want to put you to any more trouble. I'll be fine." She sneezed again.

Tyler took the mug out of her hand and pulled her up. "Come on. I'll run the water for you".

He led her through the bedroom into the ensuite bathroom. Laney shivered at his touch.

"I think you've caught a cold." He put the stopper in the huge black marble tub and added some powder as the steaming water poured and bubbles appeared everywhere. "Clean towels are in here." He pointed to a black cabinet.

"You're really very sweet to do this for me, Tyler. Thank you." Her chocolate brown eyes held the silvery grey of his until, seconds later, he gave her a quick nod, turned around and left the room, closing the door behind him.

It didn't take Laney more than a minute to strip down and climb into the massive tub. She decided if she couldn't be snowed in at home, this wasn't such a bad place to be for one night. As long as it was only one night. Tyler Hammond was a very attractive man and she already felt curiously drawn to him. That kiss he'd given her just about shot her socks off and sent her already erratic senses searching for shelter. She shook her head. No, that mustn't happen. She would not let herself become attracted to another arrogant, self-centred man again. After all, the only thing they'd done since meeting, besides sharing that overpowering kiss, was argue. Yet thinking about it, she found that oddly exhilarating. She'd never before been with a man who was willing to enter into a verbal battle with her, other than her dad and brothers. No. Forget it. No more relationships. Not after the one that exploded tonight.

Laney let the hot water thaw her fingers and toes and soothe her taut muscles. Her anger and frustration over the entire day's ordeal eased somewhat, and it wasn't long before she warmed up. Tired and now quite hungry, she finally got out of the tub and hurriedly dried herself off. After putting on her jeans, she reached for a sweater, inadvertently picking up Tyler's instead of her own. Holding it to her face she allowed the compelling musky scent hidden in the wool to surround her, rekindling the memory of their astounding kiss. Without a second thought, she pulled his sweater over her head, drained the tub and straightened up the room.

Before leaving, she glanced in the mirror that took up one full wall of the huge bathroom. She took a closer look at her face, and wasn't at all pleased with what she saw. Her make-up was practically non-existent owing to the snow and wind, and the steam from her bath. And her hair looked terrible, the long ends were soaked. She towelled it dry as best she could, then ran a comb through it, deciding that was as good as she could manage tonight.

When she went into the living room Tyler was busy in the kitchen. The delicious aroma of sizzling steak filled the air, and music was playing, a soft jazz melody with a hypnotic saxophone solo. The lights were dimmer too, allowing the snowy city scene to engulf the room.

"Feeling better?" He smiled.

"Yes, thanks. And warmer, too." She walked into the kitchen. "Can I give you a hand?"

"Have a seat. Dinner's nearly ready. I hope you like steak, and I've found enough fresh veggies for a salad. Will that do?"

"Sounds delicious. Are you sure I can't do anything?"

Tyler looked around. "You could set the table. Knives and forks and things are in those drawers." He pointed.

Laney set about her task. It fascinated her that everything right down to the telephone, the tub, and the knives and forks were either red, black or white. She commented on this.

Tyler grinned. "You find it boring?"

"Not at all." She shook her head unable to find the right word. "Very...dramatic. Very bold. I like it."

"Dinner's ready. Have a seat."

They both sat down, Laney facing the window so she could watch the snow fall. She took a bite of the steak and instantly realized how hungry she was. Tyler was ravenous, too, and they finished their meal in record time, leaving little room for conversation.

After they'd finished, Laney rose and gathered their plates. Tyler put his hand on her arm to stop her. "What are you doing?"

"I'm going to do the dishes. I noticed you don't have a dishwasher."

"I'll do them, Laney."

"No, you made dinner. I'll clean up."

"Why don't we both do them? Do you want to wash or dry?"

"I'll wash." Laney pushed up the sleeves of the sweater and ran the hot water. "Where did you learn to cook like that? My steak was perfect."

"One of my many hidden talents." Tyler was beside her now drying the clean plates. She could feel his body swaying to the rhythm of the music, and out of the corner of her eye she noticed he had taken off his sweater and unfastened the first few buttons of his navy blue shirt. Beneath lay deeply tanned skin covered in a mat of dark, curly hair. It unnerved her that she should be concentrating more on Tyler's body than the dirty plate in her hand, and she jolted back to reality when he spoke.

"Tell me about yourself, Laney."

"What do you want to know?"

They had finished the dishes now and as Tyler put the last few things away, Laney dried her hands and wandered over to the living room window which, like the bedroom window, spanned the entire wall. Through the frosted glass she observed the snowy Toronto skyline.

"I've never seen the city like this before. Your view is absolutely mesmerising. And the snow makes it even more beautiful."

Tyler came over to join her, sharing the view. "It's marvellous, isn't it? One of the main reasons I bought this place." Again, Laney shivered, and not from the cold.

"Here, let's sit by the fire." He steered her over to the sofa. "Would you like another mug of tea?"

"No, thanks. I'm fine."

"You didn't answer my question."

"What question?"

"Who are you, Laney Calderone?"

She took a deep, relaxed breath. "I'm a tired and warm lost soul. And what about you?"

"I'm a tired, stuffed, Good Samaritan." He smiled and sat down beside her. "When you're ready to go to sleep, let me know. I'll stay in the guest room and you can have the master bedroom."

"No, I'm not going to push you from your own bed, Tyler. I'm the guest, I'll take the guest room, or even here on the sofa would be fine."

"Laney, please. This is my home and I want you to sleep in the master bedroom. Now, isn't there a phone call you need to make to let someone know where you are and that you're safe? My laptop is in the study if you'd rather send an email, to let someone know you're all right."

Laney thought for a time, then shook her head. "No. There's no one I need to contact."

"No one?" His eyes narrowed. "Laney, somebody must be worrying, wondering where you are and if you're safe."

"Let them." She held his gaze for a moment, then put her head on his shoulder and closed her eyes. The delicious meal, the soft music and the warm fire all combined to make her very sleepy.

"Laney..." She heard a whisper and her head rolled gently back onto the sofa. Her eyes fluttered open to see Tyler standing in front of her. He smiled. "I think we should call it a night." He held out his hand to help her up.

"I'll sleep here, Tyler. I'm halfway there already." She closed her eyes again.

"Oh no you don't. Come on." He leaned over and without effort gathered her into his arms. She opened her eyes to find him carrying her into the bedroom.

"Tyler..."

"Laney, shut up," he said gently. He lowered her onto the huge bed and covered her with the white furry blanket. He disappeared then returned with a woolly afghan which he placed over her feet. Laney was only vaguely aware of what he was doing, sleep consuming her.

"Goodnight, Laney. Sweet dreams."

# Chapter 3

Laney woke the next morning unsure where she was. She propped herself up on her elbows and stared at the red, black and white surroundings, the broken shards of crystal still sprinkled around the fireplace, and the unfamiliar bed she was lying on. Right, now she remembered. Stranded because of the snowstorm. With Tyler.

She glanced at her watch and discovered she had slept too late. She must get out of Tyler's home, she'd invaded his privacy long enough.

As she walked into the bathroom she thought of how easily she had adapted to staying here. His condo was so comfortable, so peaceful. She peeled off her clothes and stepped into the enormous shower stall beside the huge tub she'd soaked in last night.

After a quick invigorating shower, she dressed, again choosing Tyler's sweater over her own. The wool was warm against her skin and the powerful scent of his cologne remained, assailing her senses anew.

As she brushed her hair, her tummy grumbled. A cup of very hot, very strong tea or coffee was what she needed right now. She stepped quietly into the living room, thinking Tyler might still be asleep, but to her surprise he was already up, and the heavenly aroma of freshly brewed coffee reached her.

"Morning." He greeted her with a smile. "Hungry?"

"Good morning. Yes, I am."

"Did you sleep well?"

"Yes, thanks. You?"

"Oh, I never have trouble sleeping. Coffee?"

"Sounds good." She joined him in the kitchen and couldn't help noticing how the deep teal shirt he was wearing made his grey eyes even more silvery, if that were possible.

He poured the steaming liquid into two mugs and handed her one. "What would you like for breakfast?" he asked.

"Thanks," she took the mug and sat down. "What would you suggest?"

"I haven't done any grocery shopping recently, so I'm sorry but the choices are limited. We could have eggs, eggs or eggs. What would you prefer?"

Laney laughed. "How about eggs?"

"Ah, the perfect choice, Madam. Our chef will prepare them in whatever style you like as long as it's either boiled, scrambled, or broken."

"Broken?"

"Omelettes, Madam."

She sipped the delicious coffee. "Are you always this happy in the morning?"

"Madam has again answered my question with a question, and at this rate, it will be lunch time before we eat."

Laney put down her mug and stood up. "Why doesn't Sir enjoy his coffee and Madam will make the breakfast, seeing as Sir made the excellent dinner last night?" Tyler's spirit had caught Laney, lifting her into his world. And she was enjoying her visit.

Tyler stepped back pretending to be astonished. "Madam can cook?"

"Certainly! What did you think, Sir, that I was just another pretty face?"

Tyler sat down. "Oh, no," he said in a voice very different from the one he had used to joke around. "Far more than that, Madam, far more than that."

Laney got to work preparing the omelettes. Tyler's fridge was certainly not full, however, she managed to find some Havarti and cheddar cheeses, then noticed half a Spanish onion and a red pepper, some of the leftovers from last night's salad. There were also a few mushrooms that looked like they'd seen fresher days. She gave them a cautionary sniff, decided to chance it, and chopped them up and tossed them into the mixture.

Tyler, finishing his coffee, got up and glanced out of the window. "Would you believe it's still snowing?"

She looked up. "Has it been snowing all night?" A surge of uneasiness overwhelmed Laney's thoughts as she realized she might be trapped here longer than she had originally expected — or wanted.

"Let's find out." Tyler punched a few buttons on a remote control, and the room filled with music.

"Breakfast is served," Laney said.

As they sat down to eat, the sharp voice of a radio announcer broke the silence. "Good morning, Toronto! Yes, it's hard to believe it's only the middle of November, but we're in the midst of a whopping great hit from Mother Nature, and she hasn't finished with us yet. Over sixteen inches of the white stuff is already here and another major system will hit us in the next twenty-four hours bringing lots more to shovel. Full details on the weather coming up. In other news..."

Tyler pushed a button and the room went quiet. "Laney, what is it?"

Laney was motionless, a forkful of omelette paused halfway to her mouth. "I'm stuck here, aren't I?" she whispered. "How can I even think of asking you to take me home with all the snow still coming down?"

"Why don't you finish your breakfast? Then we'll find a way to get you home," he paused, "if you really want to go."

Laney examined his steely eyes, which held her gaze for a long while, then he resumed eating. "What do you mean, if I really want to go?"

He shrugged. "After I persuaded you to stay here last night, you certainly weren't in any hurry to contact your family or friends to let them know where you were and that you were safe. Which tells me that you don't really want to go home. At least not right now."

She rubbed her forehead, feeling a headache coming on. Was it the stress of being in this situation, or frustration that he'd described her thoughts and feelings so precisely? Thoughts and feelings she was unwilling to admit. "No, you're wrong. I have to go home. Don't you want me out of your way? Haven't I done enough to disrupt your life? This snowstorm has certainly upset my plans."

Tyler swallowed his last bite of toast. "Laney, don't take everything so personally. I'm sure the snow didn't fall just to disrupt your life." He grinned.

"Be honest, I *have* disrupted your life, Tyler, haven't I? I know it would drive me crazy, having a total stranger stay in my home! It's such an intrusion!"

"I'm not you, Laney, and you're not an intrusion. And, even if you were, not all intrusions are unwanted."

"Meaning?"

"Meaning if you don't hurry up and eat, your omelette will be cold, then you'll be homeless and hungry. Why don't you finish up while I wash the dishes?"

Laney watched as Tyler took his plate into the kitchen, her thoughts racing to find a way to get out of this man's life. He was being kind when he said those things, although he'd hit the nail on the head when he said she didn't want to go home right now. It wasn't that she wanted to stay here...was it? No, it was because she wasn't ready to face her family and share with them the momentous news of her pregnancy and broken engagement. But she knew she was an unwelcome intrusion in Tyler's life, no matter what he said, and she should try to find a way home. No use calling family, they wouldn't venture out in this weather for her and although she knew the city fairly well she had no clear idea exactly where she was. And getting to her car wouldn't help her get home. She'd have to get it towed when the storm broke. Whenever that would be.

VICTORIA GRANT

"Not hungry?" Tyler looked down at her half-eaten breakfast.

"Sorry."

He took her plate. "Would you like another cup of coffee?"

"No, thanks."

"Laney, I meant what I said about you being here. You're not in my way, please stop thinking that you are."

She managed a smile. "I know you don't want me here, Tyler."

"Don't tell me what I want and don't want, Laney." His voice was harsh. "I invited you here for a reason and having heard there's more snow on the way, I can hardly expect you to find your way home today. You can stay as long as you want. I mean that."

"Seems I have no choice in the matter, but I'll be out of your way as soon as I can." She got up and headed for the bedroom.

"You talk as if you're an intrusion. You're not."

"How can you say that? You just said I interrupted your life."

"I said not all intrusions are unwanted. There's a difference."

"Well, I think I should make a few phone calls. Perhaps someone can come for me." Laney closed the bedroom door behind her. Even though Tyler had tried to dismiss her doubts, she knew she was in his way. He lived alone and liked his privacy. Her being here was not allowing him to enjoy it. She knew she would feel inconvenienced in so many ways if a stranger came along one day and happened to get snowed in with her. Besides, her conscience was gnawing at her, demanding that she find a way to get home. After the events of last night, she had a ton of thinking and explaining to do.

As she sat on the bed and stared at the phone, she knew there was no one she could call. She had lots of friends but none she could ask to make a perilous journey through the mounting snow, and at this moment, she was not up to asking a favour from any member of her family. She was, whether she liked it or not, stuck here until the storm passed. Chalk another one up to karma.

After a while, when Laney had freshened up a bit, and had given Tyler some breathing space, she went into the kitchen to make a cup of tea. She glanced around the room, he was nowhere in sight.

"Tyler?" she called out. "Tyler, where are you?"

"Right here," he shouted from the hallway.

She walked over to see him tugging on his boots.

"Where are you going? You're not taking me home, are you?" She surprised herself when she detected a note of disappointment in her voice. She hoped Tyler hadn't caught it.

"I'm going for food. If the snow continues for a few days, we'll need groceries. I thought I'd brave the elements and walk to a shop a block from here. The owner and his wife live above the store. They're always open and they'll have what we need. I won't be long." He pulled on a heavy overcoat.

"I'll come, too." Laney put on her jacket.

"There's no need for both of us to get soaked, Laney. You stay here in the warmth. I'll be back in a little while."

Laney stepped into her boots. "No, I want to come."

"Are you sure? The snow is really coming down out there."

"I'm sure. I could use the fresh air."

"I think you'll get more fresh air than you bargained for in that tiny ski jacket. You need a warmer coat." He opened the closet door. "Put this on. It'll protect you from the wind." He tossed her a heavy navy duffle coat.

Laney stared at him in defiance for a few seconds, knowing he was right. She remained silent, not wanting to give him the satisfaction of admitting it out loud. She slowly took off her ski jacket and put on the coat while Tyler waited patiently by the door. The coat nearly reached her feet and weighed a ton, yet she knew it would keep her warm, and she smiled as she caught a whiff of the same beguiling scent, a disarming reminder of the coat's owner, lingering in the collar. "Ready."

"Let's go." Tyler locked the door behind them and they travelled in silence.

As Tyler had well described, the icy winds immediately took their breath away as soon as they stepped outside, and Laney tightened her grip on the collar to shield her from the bitter cold. Heavy, wet flakes fell all around them, swirling and dancing in front of their faces. Their boots crunched the snow underfoot and they made very slow progress. The streets were almost empty, no cars, buses, taxi cabs. No pedestrians either, except a woman walking her dog, and a few kids having fun building a snow fort on the sidewalk. Everyone was home waiting for the storm to pass.

When they finally stepped inside the store, Laney heard a small bell tinkling as she lowered the collar and shook her head, ridding herself of flakes that had found a temporary home. "This is incredible!"

"Sure is somethin', ain't it, Missy?" a friendly voice cried out from behind the counter. "Ah! It's Mr. Hammond! How ye doin' today?"

"Hello, Duncan. You're looking well." Tyler shook his hand after removing a wet glove. "Not too busy today, I take it."

"Aye, this weather, Mr. Hammond. Not a good day fer men or monsters!" Duncan ran a hand through his thick mass of ginger curls. "What can I be gettin' fer ye today?"

"I thought I'd better stock up, Duncan, in case this stuff lasts until May."

Duncan chuckled. "Ye never know, laddie, ye never know!"

Laney had busied herself wandering up and down the aisles. Tyler had been in no hurry to introduce her to Duncan, so she kept busy by taking mental inventory of the shelves, which contained everything from pet food and string to blankets and batteries. It was a general store in every sense of the word.

"Laney, where are you?" Tyler called out.

She popped her head around a corner. "Right here."

"I need your help. I'm useless at this. I can think of a hundred and one things when I'm in the kitchen but as soon as I get in the store, my mind goes blank. And I never bother to make a list. So, where shall we start?"

Laney smiled at Duncan as he handed her a basket. "Where would you suggest we start, Duncan?" she asked.

He chuckled again, took off his wire-rimmed glasses, rubbed them with his apron, then set them on the edge of his nose. "Well, I'll tell ye, Missy, if I were snowed in with a lovely lassie like ye, I'd not be thinkin' 'bout food!"

Laney blushed profusely as Tyler laughed. "What would Emma say if she heard that, Duncan?"

"She'd be prayin' we'd be snowed under t'ree 'undred an' sixty-five days of the year, she would!" Duncan thumped the counter with his fist and threw back his head in laughter.

The door opened, the bell tinkled again and another wet customer entered. "You two be findin' what ye need. I'll be with ye in a wee minute or two." Duncan patted Laney on the shoulder, then wandered over to help the new arrival.

After twenty minutes of exploring the shelves they had filled the basket with milk, cereal, soup, bread, tea and coffee, and because Duncan even had a small produce section, they picked up some fresh fruit and salad ingredients. Then Laney found the 'Sweets and Treats' shelves, where Tyler learned very quickly that he wouldn't be leaving the store in one piece unless her favourite chocolate came home with them.

"Isn't this an awful lot of chocolate for two people?" he frowned.

"Two? Oh, you like chocolate, too?"

"Evidently, not as much as you. Okay, you enjoy the chocolate, I'll go get my favourite ice cream."

"Works for me."

Finally, Tyler took the basket to the counter where Duncan was finishing with the other customer.

"Aye, so ye found what ye be needin', 'ave ye?" he asked, emptying the basket.

"I think this will do us for a while, don't you, Laney?"

She silently nodded, hesitant to speak or make eye contact with Duncan again, for fear he'd come out with another embarrassing remark.

Duncan rang in all the items. "I hope, laddie, that ye have a nice bottle or two o' wine at 'ome! Ye can't be 'avin' a romantic dinner with the snow a fallin' an' the wind a howlin' without sum bubbly!"

Laney, the colour returning to her cheeks, headed for the door.

Tyler grinned and paid for the groceries. "Take care, my friend. See you again soon." He held the door open and Laney rapidly darted through it into the frigid air.

An easy grin creasing his face, Tyler caught up to her. "What's your hurry?"

"It's cold."

"It wasn't in the store."

Laney shrugged and kept moving.

"I'm sorry if Duncan embarrassed you, Laney. He doesn't mean any harm by it. It's his way. He's a dear friend."

"I wasn't embarrassed."

"No?"

"No. Why should I be embarrassed?"

"Then why did you turn five shades of scarlet?"

Laney ignored his question and moved even faster into the driving snow. "Can we get back? My feet are freezing."

Once home, after all the groceries had been put away, Tyler poured himself a stiff drink. "Would you like one?"

Laney was sitting by the fire glancing through a magazine, nibbling on some chocolate. "No thanks, not right now."

Tyler sat down opposite her. "So, tell me something, Laney. Why were you in that part of town last night? What were you doing?"

Laney put aside the magazine. "Why?"

"I'm curious. There aren't too many homes near there. It's mostly a business area with no restaurants or theatres."

"I could ask you the same question."

"Go ahead."

"Okay. What were you doing there?"

"Let's say I came from a business meeting."

"Business? At midnight? What sort of business are you in, Mr. Hammond?"

Tyler ignored her question and finished his drink. "Your turn."

"I could use a tea." She dashed into the kitchen.

He followed and sat at the table watching her. "It's all right if you don't want to tell me, Laney. It's none of my business."

Laney reached for the sugar bowl but as she grasped it, a sudden sneeze caught her off guard and the bowl slipped from her hand and fell to the floor, sending crystals cascading everywhere. She turned and routed noisily through the cutlery drawer. "Don't you have any teaspoons in this place?"

After finally finding a spoon, she searched for the tea. When she opened the cupboard door, two cereal boxes fell from the crowded shelf onto the counter and a package of rice hit her on the head, burst open and exploded all over the floor.

"Shit!" Having never been tackled by groceries before, Laney leaned against the counter, sighed heavily, and counted to ten.

"Problem?" Tyler hid a smirk.

"Nope." She wasn't going to let trivial things like sugar or rice or Tyler Hammond get the better of her.

"Fine." He got up and walked away.

Laney watched his back as he went to the bar and poured himself another drink. It was a simple question he'd asked her, one she shouldn't be upset about answering. He was naturally curious why she was out alone that late and, she supposed, it warranted an answer. Yet she was not ready to reveal that when they met was a split second after her life, as she had known it, had blown up around her. And even though he seemed irritated that she hadn't told him, he was right when he said it was none of his business.

She replaced the cereal boxes and finally found the tea. This time she was able to prepare a mug without being attacked by any rogue provisions, then sat near the window feeling a little calmer. "Where do you keep your broom? I'll clean up the mess."

"Leave it." Tyler was sitting by the fire reading.

"No, I made the mess, I'll clean it —"

"I said leave it!" he snapped.

Laney frowned. Why was he angry? Surely he wasn't getting upset over the sugar and rice being spilled? No, she thought, it must be her refusal to divulge last night's activities. Well, too bad, it was still none of his business.

They sat for a long while, an uncomfortable atmosphere permeating the room. Laney watched the snow cover the city, Tyler read by the fire.

Laney's stomach was not reacting well to the hot tea, or was it all the chocolate she'd eaten? She felt queasy again and decided she wanted to go home. It wasn't a good idea to stay here. She had to at least *try* to get home and she wondered if one of her family wouldn't consider it too much aggravation to come to her rescue. Maybe her brother Jamie's SUV could handle the road conditions.

"I'm going to make a phone call," she said, as she walked past him on her way to the bedroom. "Maybe even try the taxi cabs again."

"Laney!" Tyler called out to her. "Where do you think you're going?"

His sudden outburst startled her and she spun around. "I told you. I'm going to call my family or try the taxis again. I don't feel well and I need to be home."

"Laney, don't be a fool. You've been staring out of that window for the last hour, you can see for yourself nothing is moving on the streets. We barely made it to the shop on foot. You don't think a car would make it all the way from Forest Hill and back in this stuff, do you?"

"Well, I have to do something! I can't stay here any longer."

"Why not?" He raised a mocking eyebrow. "Didn't you want the rice for dinner? You could've just told me instead of scattering the grains all over the kitchen floor."

Her lips tightened. "I'm sorry about that, it was an accident. And I'll clean it up if you tell me where you keep your broom."

"I said leave it."

"Fine, I'll leave it," she sighed. "This isn't working, Tyler. I'm in your way. You know it. I know it. Me being here is not a good idea."

"When did you *ever* think it was? If I recall, I had to talk you into it for fear you'd die of exposure if I let you out of my sight!"

Laney's temper accelerated at light speed to its boiling point. "Not *this* again! What is it with you? An overabundance of testosterone that makes you so obnoxious?" Laney planted her hands firmly on her hips. "I can't believe you think I'm so damned helpless! I would've found a way home if you hadn't wandered by last night. I'm not an idiot, I do have some brains!"

"Then why the *hell* aren't you using them now? You know you can't leave here in this weather, especially since you've gotten sick with a cold. You're staying put. End of discussion."

"Don't tell me what to do! You're not my father!"

"No, but you obviously need someone to discipline you. You've probably gotten away with being a spoilt little brat most of your life!"

Laney's eyes narrowed. "What's this now? You think you know all about me and all the things I've ever done in my life? After knowing me for less than twenty-four hours? Are you psychic or is that the alcohol talking?"

"Listen, Cinderella, here's a scoop for you. Take notes. You're not leaving until the snow stops. Discussion over."

"Well, here's a scoop for *you*, Mr. Hammond. You have *no right* to tell me what to do! I'm leaving. Now." Laney spun around and marched into the bedroom, slamming the French doors behind her.

Tyler stormed in after her. "Who do you think you are?" his booming voice shattering the snowy silence. "Like it or not, woman, this is *my* home and I don't like the way you're treating it or me! I realize this is not the ideal situation for either of us, but for God's sake, let's at least try to be civil to one another!"

Laney perched on the edge of the bed listening to his tirade. She leisurely crossed her legs, her foot drawing slow circles in the air. She calmly gazed at the ceiling, waiting for him to finish. "Are you quite through?" she asked, giving him her favourite honey sweet smile, knowing it was risking another display of his anger, but she was beyond caring.

"You, Laney Calderone, are nothing but a spoilt, stubborn, self-absorbed prima donna!"

"And you, Tyler Hammond, are nothing but an arrogant, insufferable, condescending bastard!"

"I knew I should have gone with my second instinct and kept right on walking when I saw you last night."

"I wish you had!"

Instantly he was in front of her. "Perhaps I should forget I'm a gentleman and toss you out of here right now and let you fend for yourself!" He sneered. "Then we'd soon see how strong and independent you really are!"

"You wouldn't dare!"

"Let's get one thing straight, Miss Calderone. This storm has given you no choice other than to stay here. But be assured, the instant this snow stops, I plan to personally take you back to your car and fix the damned thing myself! Then we'll never have to see each other *ever again*! And that should make both of us *very* happy!" He left the room, closing the doors softly behind him.

Tyler swore as he strode into his study determined to get some work done. However, after only a few minutes, he realized he couldn't concentrate on the files in front of him and was in no mood to try. A large brandy might help ease his frustration and get Laney off his mind, at least for a short while, because having this exasperating woman in his home, for God knows how much longer, was sorely testing his patience.

Tyler had been raised to be a gentleman, his parents had taught him having a high standard of integrity, along with decency and good manners, would benefit him in all areas of his life. Accordingly, he'd done what he thought was right in assisting Laney last night. So why was she treating him like he'd kidnapped her and was thoroughly enjoying torturing her with cruel and bizarre punishments? Was she *trying* to drive him crazy? Did she get some perverse pleasure seeing him lose his temper? Why couldn't she see their predicament for what it was, and at least meet him half way, so they could try to get along with each other?

I don't need this kind of drama at my age, he thought. Okay, I'm not ready for a pipe and slippers yet, I know thirty-two isn't over the hill. But is it too much to ask for a reasonably tranquil life, a successful business and a fair divorce settlement? None of which are going to happen any time soon, with Tracy digging up such ridiculous and irrelevant issues with the divorce, and my biggest client dropping me for no reason and returning to my competitor. No, it has not been a good week. And if that's not enough BS to deal with, now I have this stunningly beautiful yet infuriating woman stranded here with me until the snow stops! Some days it just doesn't pay to be a nice guy.

# Chapter 4

A few hours later, Laney emerged from the bedroom. Tyler, she noticed, was sitting by the fire reading. She walked directly past him and into the kitchen, determined to search until she found a broom to clean up the mess she'd made earlier. As she entered the kitchen, she noticed the clean-up she had been planning had already been done. The kitchen, including the floor, was sugar and rice-free.

She made another cup of tea and sat at the smoked glass dining table to watch the snow fall. She was again astounded at how beautiful the view was. The snow swirled over the lake, barely perceptible in the dim light. She had always loved a snowfall in the city, so peaceful, so soft, perfectly blanketing rooftops, sidewalks, trees and cars. And it was a completely different city from this view. No family squabbles, no business pressures or personal worries, no politics, and no noise. She closed her eyes imagining how wonderful a world like this could be.

"Laney?" Tyler's voice was a whisper. "Are you okay?"

She opened her eyes to find him sitting across the table from her. "I'm sorry about the mess in the kitchen, Tyler. I was going to clean it up."

"Forget it. Laney, I'm sorry we fought. It's pointless to go on arguing, don't you think? I mean neither one of us can do anything about this situation. We should get to know each other a little and at least try to be friends."

She nodded. "You're right. I'm sorry I'm such a self-absorbed prima donna."

A slight smile creased his face. "I said that in anger, Laney. I'm sorry. I didn't mean it."

"You're right, though. I am when I don't get my own way. I guess that's what happens when you have parents too busy to worry about you, and four older brothers who torment you mercilessly."

"*Four* older brothers?" Tyler winced.

Laney nodded. "Yep, not even one sister to share with or confide in."

"Sisters aren't always great. I have one I'd trade in for a brother any time."

"Is she older than you?"

"Younger. Katy always puts money ahead of family, so it's difficult for us to find common ground. I haven't seen or heard from her in over a year, and as our parents died years ago, I'm it for my family."

"That must get lonely sometimes." Laney finished her tea.

"Sometimes." Tyler paused to watch the snow. "Katy sided with my wife when I filed for divorce," he finally continued. "She thought I had been the one at fault, the one not trying hard enough to make the marriage work. Now she totally ignores me."

"I'm sorry."

Tyler smiled. "I consider it a blessing without the disguise."

"How long were you married?"

"Four years. Not long, really. We both knew it was a mistake almost from the beginning. Tracy and I were chums in high school, we dated in university, then foolishly took the next step and got married." Tyler swallowed the last of his brandy. "In fact, that's where I was last night before we met." He smiled. "I met with my lawyer who told me things are not going too well at all with my divorce and that's how my phone shattered. I threw it in a fit of temper. What about you, Laney, are you married?"

"No, I'm not." Her face clouded over and she stared at the drops of tea in the bottom of her mug. She realized he'd forgotten their conversation in the car last night and his surly reaction to her single status.

She looked up at him. "I was engaged to be married; however, that ended rather abruptly. Last night, as a matter of fact." She rubbed her finger where a five-carat diamond solitaire had once rested.

"Sorry, I didn't mean to remind you of it."

She shrugged. "It's okay. It was the right thing to do. I don't know anyone these days who has a happy marriage. Most of my friends and co-workers are either single, separated or divorced."

"What about your brothers?"

"All single."

"Your parents are together, aren't they?"

"Together, yes, but I've sometimes wondered if they're happily married. My mother, the 'Queen of High Society', spends all her time organizing charity balls, visiting the underprivileged, and finding new ways to get on my nerves. And although I work with my dad, we don't spend as much time as I'd like together. He's too busy trying to find a new company to buy and making sure his tax shelters don't disappear.

"Calderone Industries?"

"That's us."

"I thought your name sounded familiar. I've had dealings with your company on occasion. I know your brother Stephen."

"What is it you do, Tyler?"

"I'm an Investment Advisor. I used to work for one of the city's largest investment firms, but the daily grind and constant BS got to be too much. I quit and started my own company, which enables me to work from home a lot, it's a welcome change."

They sat quietly for a long time watching the endless white falling from the sky.

"I want to show you something." Tyler got up from the table and walked to the door and put on his coat and boots. "Come on."

"Finally had enough of me and you're taking me home?"

"Nope. Grab that coat and come with me."

Laney did as he said and followed Tyler into the hallway. As they got into the elevator, Laney asked, "We're not going outside again, are we?"

"We're nearly there."

She noticed Tyler had pressed the button for the top floor of the building. They stepped out of the elevator and he led her down a long hall to a side door.

"What are we doing?"

"Patience, Laney, patience."

Tyler propelled her gently through the door into a crowded little storage room until they came to a flight of stairs.

She turned, a questioning look on her face. Tyler pointed. "Keep going."

Laney climbed, and when she reached the top, she tried to open the heavy door, but a gust of wind blew her back inside. Tyler stepped beside her and thrust the door open.

"The roof! We're on the roof?" she exclaimed, barely able to breathe with the gale force winds blowing around her. "Tyler, what are we doing up here? *Trying* to catch pneumonia?"

"I want to show you something." He gently took her arm and cautiously, amidst the snow and wind, led her close to the edge.

"Tyler!" she shrieked. "Don't!" she shut her eyes tight.

"You have to see this, Laney. The city is magnificent from this view."

"I can't look, I'll be sick!"

Tyler chuckled. "You'll be fine. Take a deep breath and open your eyes. I won't let go of you."

She felt him step behind her, his sturdy arms tightened around her waist and Laney slowly opened her eyes. She looked down nervously, frightened at first, then she relaxed as she took in the breathtaking view. Even though the howling wind and biting cold surrounded her, she felt an inner peace and contentment she had never imagined possible. Tyler carefully guided her to the other side of the building where the wind wasn't as strong.

"You're forty-five stories high. Incredible, isn't it?"

"It's beautiful," she whispered, taken in by the view. "I've never been on a rooftop before." She tucked some wind-blown strands of hair behind her ears. "Do you come here often?" She grinned.

"Yes, I do. I can breathe up here, clear my head. I find it's one of the few places where I can unwind. I know it sounds odd, but this is my private sanctuary. On a clear night, I can see into tomorrow." Tyler took a deep breath and Laney watched as a tranquil air seemed to cloak him, the calm evident on his face, and she felt privileged that he wanted her to share his special refuge.

Laney, now more confident in her footing, carefully moved a little closer to the edge and searched the skyline. "Toronto is such a beautiful city. It's hard to appreciate when you're on the ground in the middle of it."

Tyler nodded. "There's nothing like a different view to give you a new perspective on things." He reached down and gathered a handful of snow.

Laney was captivated watching the barely visible twinkling lights from the CN Tower and finding other familiar landmarks, she didn't notice Tyler backing away from her. A clump of wet snow struck her shoulder.

"Gotcha!" Tyler smiled, forming another snowball in his gloved hands.

"Hey! No fair!" Laney turned to chase him but not knowing the roof as well as he did, she lost him when Tyler hid behind one of the many air conditioning units.

"Coward!" she shouted, preparing her own snowball. She stepped about noiselessly, trying to discover his hiding spot. She heard a sound and turned as another flying projectile hit her arm.

"Gotcha again!"

This time Laney ran after him and managed to toss her snowball, catching his back as he turned away.

"Gotcha back!" She laughed and turned to run but she slipped suddenly on a patch of ice and fell face down into a snow drift. Tyler appeared instantly and kneeled down beside her.

"Laney, are you okay?"

She was silent, motionless.

"Laney." There was panic in his voice. He reached out to touch her shoulder and she slowly rolled over, her eyes closed. "Laney! Speak to me! Are you all right?"

She opened her eyes and smiled, at the same time hurling the snowball she'd been hiding in her hand directly into Tyler's face.

"Gotcha again!" She giggled and stood up swiftly, brushing the snow from her jeans.

"Find that funny, do you?" Tyler wiped the melting snow off his face. "You'll pay for that, woman!"

Laney started to run. "Not unless you can catch me!"

Tyler chased her around the rooftop, finally overtaking her near the door where they had come in. Laney leaned against the wall trying to catch her breath. He stood in front of her patting the snow in his hands firmly into another sphere. An evil grin appeared on his face.

She glanced at the snowball, then into his silvery eyes. "What are you going to do with that?"

"I believe you got the last shot. That makes it my turn."

Laney tried to edge sideways along the wall. "I've had enough. Let's go inside. It's too cold up here."

"Not so fast, Miss Calderone. You don't think you can get away from me that easily, do you?" Tyler took a step closer and positioned his free hand directly above her shoulder, smiling all the while.

Laney's back was forced up against the wall now, Tyler's solid form moved even closer, providing her with no chance to flee. Her body trembled, either from the harsh wind or Tyler's close proximity. While she endeavoured to devise an escape plan, she couldn't help but meticulously examine the stubble forming on his cheek, the few unruly curls of chest hair peeping out of his coat, and the strength and smoothness of his jaw line. She was more than a little curious how soft and warm that spot behind his right ear lobe would feel to her lips.

Their eyes finally met and a deep throbbing ache originating in the pit of her stomach sent shock waves hurtling through her. Laney turned away and closed her eyes, attempting to return her breathing to normal. She felt like a powder keg waiting for that one spark to ignite within her.

She opened her eyes to find Tyler still watching her. His lips parted as if he were about to speak, then he turned his head and swore under his breath.

Laney watched him, saying nothing, not trusting the sound of her voice.

It seemed like eons later when he let the snowball drop from his hand and finally spoke, his voice rough and uneven. "Let's go."

After a silent elevator ride, they rid themselves of wet coats and boots, and Tyler turned on a few lights. It was mid-afternoon and the condo had darkened considerably, a sure sign the snow would continue to fall.

"Are you hungry?" he asked.

"Not really."

"No? I thought with you not finishing your breakfast you'd be ravenous by now. I am." He went into the kitchen and opened a cupboard door.

Laney joined him. "Well, now that you mention it, I guess I could go for something. What do you suggest?"

Their eyes met again, and Laney turned away feeling a sudden and inexplicable nervous energy between them.

Tyler cleared his throat. "How does a mug of hot soup and a sandwich sound?"

"Perfect. And I wouldn't mind another cup of tea."

They moved about the kitchen, trying not to get in each other's way. Laney felt awkward and clumsy being so near to him. She tried in vain to figure out what it was about this man – sometimes an arrogant mass of superiority, sometimes a gentle soul of kindness - that left her struggling to make a simple pot of tea.

Just before they sat down to eat, Tyler grabbed the remote control, pushed a few buttons, and the same upbeat jazz melody Laney had heard the night before filled the room.

"Your favourite tune?" she asked.

He nodded. "Tracy hated it. It reminds me of all the things I'll achieve when our divorce is final."

"What things?"

"My freedom for a start. My home, where I can do what I want when I want, like listen to my favourite music. I bought this place when we first separated and had it decorated how I wanted. Tracy had our house done in pinks and greens. I hate pink! I love red and black. Very striking colours, don't you think? And very sexy."

Again, their eyes locked. Laney tried to look away, as a strong yet invisible bond held her in its clutches once more.

The music stopped and broke their trance. Tyler changed the CD, this time to another jazz piece and a slow, sultry rhythm now filled the room.

They finished their lunch without any conversation, just enjoying the music. Laney got up to clear away her dishes, and as she neared the counter, she felt Tyler's hand on her shoulder. She turned to see his smiling face.

"Come dance with me," he said softly. He took her hand, as his mesmerizing energy propelled her down the kitchen steps and into a dream world. Spellbound, she felt his skilful arms take control, one sliding firmly around her lower back, the other gently clasping her hand. They began to sway to the music and Laney felt his body stir and seductively caress hers as they moved effortlessly around the room, his tempting scent swirling around her. Laney closed her eyes filling her senses with this wondrous moment.

The song ended and she opened her eyes to find Tyler staring at her. He bent slightly and lowered his lips to hers.

Laney waited for her offended sense of decency to come storming through and push him away, but instead, her arms found their way around his neck, fully savouring the sensation of his strong body pressed against hers. Unlike his first kiss, which was rough and raw, this one was warm and soft. His tongue tenderly probed her mouth sending a provocative invitation to all her senses. Her knees nearly buckled as she answered his invitation. Tyler sensed her hunger, caressing her tenderly in his arms. She moaned softly and felt him shudder slightly as he moved his body closer to hers in a fascinating rhythm.

Another song began, and in one fluid motion Tyler straightened, gently pressed her head to his chest, and they continued their dance. A luscious warmth seeped into Laney's body which made melting into his arms effortless and natural. She could hear his racing heartbeat through the thin shirt, and felt the heat radiating from his body as a glorious sense of serenity enveloped her.

Then, without warning, the lights went out and the music stopped. Laney jerked herself away from Tyler's embrace.

"What's going on?" she gasped, all attempts to catch her breath unsuccessful.

"Powers gone out," he announced. "Another wonderful thing about snowstorms."

Laney stood frozen, trying to recover from their kiss. "What should we do?"

"Nothing we can do. It probably won't last too long. I think this building has a back-up generator." Tyler turned up the gas fire as Laney shivered watching him.

"Come here, Laney. Come sit by the fire and keep warm."

She moved slowly in the darkness, her way lit by the glowing embers and sparks. He reached for her hand and gently pulled her down beside him.

"What next?" she whispered nervously.

"We wait."

"That's it?"

He grinned, raising an eyebrow. "What would you like to do?"

"Shouldn't we call someone to find out what's going on?"

"I think you'll find that because the electricity has gone out, chances are the landline phones aren't working either, and as I don't have a cell anymore and yours is out of power, we're stuck."

"My God, we're trapped!"

"Yes, we have been for a while."

Laney bolted from the sofa. "No, I mean we're really trapped! The elevators won't work, will they? How will we get out of here?"

Tyler chuckled. "Laney, if the time came when you actually had to go, I'm sure the stairs would accommodate you."

"I'm not climbing down thirteen dark staircases!" A look of horror crossed her face and she paced around the room, rubbing her arms. "By the way, don't you have any candles? It's awfully dark in here."

"Candles?"

How could such a TDH be so obtuse? "Yes, candles! I'm sure you've heard of them? Wax sticks that you set fire to? Humanity has been using them for centuries on this planet! Why don't you have some on hand for an emergency like this?"

Tyler leaned back calmly folding his hands behind his head. "Where's the emergency? I don't see any emergency."

"I don't believe your attitude! Why don't you have any candles?"

"I don't like candles. They're dangerous. Besides, the fire's giving off enough light and heat. Now come sit down and keep warm."

"Stop telling me what to do! And what do you mean you don't like candles? How can you not like candles? Everybody likes candles!" She was on a roll now. An entire band of armed mercenaries couldn't stop her onslaught. "They're calming and cozy, they're fabulous little devices that come in handy for emergencies! But no, not you!! Mr. Tyler Hammond, in his infinite wisdom, can find no significant or redeeming value in them! No wonder your wife left you! How could you possibly have even one romantic evening without any candles?"

Like a caged animal, Laney paced around the room unable to compose herself. The intense energy that seared her senses when they kissed was overwhelming her, and now that the electricity had gone off, she felt anxious, every nerve ending raw and hungry.

Tyler headed to the bar and poured himself a drink. "Tracy didn't leave me, I left her. It had nothing to do with candles. And I can assure you, Miss Calderone, that when I plan a romantic evening, I certainly don't need assistance from trivial little things like candles to make that evening a success."

Laney stared at him. "I can't believe you're so calm! Not having any candles is one thing, but not getting upset over being trapped here is quite another!"

"I don't look at it as being trapped. This is my home and I'm snowed in. It's actually rather fun — or could be." He winked and saluted her with his glass.

"How can you say that?" Laney was mystified.

Tyler's brow furrowed. "Why are you so bothered by this? I'm not a homicidal maniac or a deranged psychopath! You're quite safe here alone with me." He watched her pace. "I'm beginning to understand why your fiancé dumped you."

She turned on him. "How do you know that? I didn't tell you that!"

"Not hard to figure out."

"What is that supposed to mean?"

"Nothing." Tyler sat down and flipped through a magazine. "It doesn't mean a thing."

Laney charged across the room and ripped the magazine out of his hands. "Damn you, Tyler Hammond! Tell me what you meant by that!"

He stood up swiftly, knocking her off balance and pointing his finger an inch away from her face. "You, my dear lady, have the knack of infuriating a man down to a fine art! You complain and carry on until you get your own way and you're still not satisfied when you do! It's a wonder any man could fall in love with you!" He picked up his empty glass and strode over to the bar swearing under his breath.

"I'll have you know, Mr. Hammond, that —"

"Be quiet! Please!" Tyler downed his double in one swallow and refilled the glass. "Every time we talk, we fight. Instead, let's have some peace and quiet." He brushed past her and resumed his seat by the fire, picking up the torn magazine.

Laney marched around the room taking deep breaths, trying her best to calm down. How *dare* he treat her like this! Who did he think he was? And they all said *she* had mood swings! This guy was the King of Swings! Well, Mr. Hammond, she thought, you haven't heard the last of me yet! She stormed into the bedroom and slammed the French doors behind her.

# Chapter 5

After a very restless night, Laney climbed out of bed the next morning and saw the snow still falling. "Damn." Her stomach lurched. "Am I never going to get out of this mess?"

As she stepped into the shower her thoughts drifted to Tyler. After their argument yesterday afternoon Laney had stayed in the bedroom all evening. He'd called her for dinner a few hours later, but she had declined. She was not in the mood for another round of fighting and knew Tyler could use a break from her, too.

She knew it wasn't only the fighting that kept her from joining him for dinner. She was reluctant to spend any time with him again. After that dance they shared, her feelings were chaotic. She had enjoyed it more than she first admitted to herself, feeling safe and secure in his arms. He'd taken her to a captivating realm, one where reality hovered in the background, where sounds and touches and tastes were the ultimate pleasures. She'd never experienced sensations like that, ever, and from her unexpected but stirring reactions, she knew she wanted to feel them again.

And then he'd kissed her. His lips so tender, so warm, so inviting. Laney knew she'd have to keep a tight rein on her emotions if she were to stop this wild yet wonderful connection from progressing any further. After all, it was impossible to even think about a new relationship. She'd only just been dumped by Ramone (damn Tyler for assuming that!) and she was not ready to expose her heart and soul to him so he could ride roughshod over them.

As Laney got out of the shower her stomach was doing cartwheels and she quickly dressed. After she applied a little make up and tied her hair back, she headed for the kitchen, breathing a sigh of relief when she saw that Tyler was nowhere in sight. She got busy making toast and tea, silently thanking both the back-up generator and the electric company, whichever one it was that restored the power. She picked up a magazine and sat by the fire to eat.

"Good morning."

Laney looked up to find Tyler emerging from the guest bedroom, wearing a red flannel bath robe which ended at his knees. His hair was uncombed, his face unshaven.

He noticed her gaze drifting over him. "Sorry." He tightened the belt and ran a hand through his hair. "I didn't think you'd be up yet and I'm in dire need of coffee."

Laney gulped a mouthful of hot tea, scalding her throat in the process. It took all the strength she had not to look at that solid wall of chest covered in thick, dark hair. "Don't apologize. This is your home, after all. Feel free to wander around here naked if you want to."

He raised an eyebrow. "Naked, eh? I might try it sometime."

She nearly choked on her toast. What in heaven's name had possessed her to make that moronic suggestion? Naked? Get a grip, she told herself. She could hear Tyler preparing the coffee, and she dared not look at him knowing he had little or nothing on under his robe.

"I missed you at dinner last night, Laney."

She shrugged. What could she say that hadn't already been said?

"You must be starving. Have you had breakfast?" he asked.

"I made tea and toast."

"Toast isn't breakfast. Do you want something more to eat?" He came into the room with his coffee and sat across from her, his robe parting slightly, giving Laney an intimate view of a very muscular left thigh.

"Ah...no." She tried to concentrate on his face.

"You okay?" he asked, sensing her uneasiness.

She nodded and returned to her reading.

"Laney, we need to talk." Tyler sipped from his steaming mug.

She peeked over the top of the magazine. "Again? What about this time?"

"About us."

The magazine dropped from her hands. "Us?"

"Uh huh. We seem to keep repeating the same arguments and the same apologies. We said we were going to try to get along, yet that doesn't seem to be working, does it?"

"No, it doesn't." She shook her head. "Not at all."

"What do you suggest we do about it?"

"Nothing much we can do except stay out of each other's way."

"Is that why you avoided me and stayed behind closed doors last night?"

"Tyler, you said it yesterday, whenever we talk we end up fighting, so maybe we should go our separate ways until the storm ends and I can go home and leave you in peace."

He shook his head. "That won't work."

"Why not?"

"Because this isn't a mansion, Laney. There's not enough physical space to divide between the two of us, and besides, who would get the kitchen?"

"You make it sound like a divorce settlement."

"Sorry." A tiny smile appeared on his face as he pushed his free hand through his hair again, causing his robe to slide further away from his thigh. "Do you like me, Laney?"

She frowned. "What do you mean?"

"You heard me."

"What are you —"

"Answer me."

"Okay, yes, I like you."

"I like you, too. And two people who like each other should be able to get along if they try. Doesn't that sound logical to you?"

She sighed. "Sounds great in theory, Tyler. It's when we put it into practice that we run into trouble."

"Unless we're dancing."

Laney's stomach lurched again at the memory of his powerful and responsive body swaying against hers. "We're going to dance the day away, is that what you're suggesting?"

"Do you have a better idea?"

She stared at him, trying to focus on her words, not his exquisite body. She needed to choose them very carefully. The last thing she needed was another idiotic outburst about him wandering around naked. "No, but I suggest we rethink *that* plan."

"Why?"

"Because we're not Ginger Rogers and Fred Astaire."

"How do you know? We only danced for a few minutes yesterday before the electricity went off. If it stays on today, who knows how long we could dance? And if the power goes off, I'm a great hummer."

"I think we should stay out of each other's way. That would solve our problem."

Tyler smirked. "Afraid to try my idea?"

"I don't think it's a good idea, that's all."

"Why not?"

She hesitated, unwilling to reveal her true feelings. "Because I refuse to dance with a half-naked man who hasn't bothered to shave.

"Excuses, excuses," Tyler teased. "And didn't you tell me I could wander around here naked if I wanted to? At least I have my robe on, for right now, anyway." He winked and finished his coffee, then put his mug on the kitchen counter. As he passed behind her, he gently pressed his hands into her shoulders and slowly began massaging. She instinctively lowered her head and he increased the pressure against her skin. Laney closed her eyes delighting in the tantalizing tenderness of his touch.

He leaned over and whispered in her ear, his hot breath igniting that spark within her. "I'm going to have a shave and a shower now. You make a list of your favourite dance tunes, Ginger. You know where the CD's are."

Half an hour later Tyler emerged, showered, shaven and fully clothed. Laney noticed he'd put on a black shirt and jeans, and, when he passed by her, she inhaled the intoxicating scent of his cologne that sent her senses spinning. She grabbed the nearest magazine, opened it and tried to focus on the printed words, even though they were upside down.

"Here." He tossed a light denim shirt in her direction. "You'll get warm dancing in a sweater. It'll be more comfortable."

"Thanks, but I'm in the middle of a fascinating article here and I'd like to finish it."

"Fascinating, huh? What about?" Tyler grinned, noticing Laney was 'reading' one of his financial magazines.

"About? Well, um, it's about..." Laney looked intently at the page. "It's about..." She winced and flipped it over, "Ah yes, here we are, it's about how to incorporate bond ladders into your portfolio." She smiled at him.

"Right. Riveting stuff, I'm sure. You can finish it later." He gently pulled the magazine from her hand and lifted her out of the chair.

"Tyler, this isn't a good idea." Her body trembled at his touch.

"Let's discuss it over breakfast." He propelled her into the kitchen. "What shall we have?"

"I've already eaten." She sat down.

"Toast? I think you'll be needing more than that. You didn't have any dinner last night. You must be hungry."

"No, not really."

"You're having something to eat. I'm not going to be responsible for you wasting away to nothing while you're here."

"That won't happen."

"Damn right it won't. Now, what shall we have?"

"I said I'm not hungry."

Tyler opened the fridge door and leaned against it while he took inventory of its contents. "I know, let's take advantage of the electricity while we have it and make crepes. Those fresh blueberries we got from Duncan will be perfect."

"You know how to make crepes?"

"I told you I have lots of hidden talents. And you're the lucky lady who's going to experience two of them today."

Laney frowned. "Ah...which two would these be?"

"My blueberry crepes and my Fred Astaire imitation."

"Can't wait." She winced.

"Me either." He smiled.

The crepes were delectable, as Laney knew they would be. As she finished and helped Tyler clean up the dishes, she felt a nagging ache in the pit of her stomach.

"Did you make your list of songs, Ginger?" he asked, putting the clean dishes into the cupboard.

"No. I don't want to dance, Tyler. I'm not feeling well." Laney sat down by the fire, nausea now gripping her.

"More excuses, Laney?" He sat down across from her. "No, I'm not well."

"Scared of a little waltz —" Tyler stopped short when he became aware of how sick she looked. Her skin was pale, her hands trembled, and beads of perspiration were congregating on her forehead.

"I need to lie down for a while, I think." She put her head back and took a few deep breaths.

"Let me get you some water." Tyler dashed into the kitchen and returned with the glass. He helped her sit up and she sipped the cool liquid.

"You've not been well since you got here. I think the flu has finally hit you."

"Maybe." Laney lay silent, her head throbbing. Suddenly, her stomach lurched and she bolted and ran for the bathroom.

Minutes later she emerged and Tyler reached for her arm as she walked unsteadily to the sofa and sat down.

"Do you want me to call a doctor, Laney?"

"No, I'll be fine." She closed her eyes trying desperately to get her emotional and physical states in order. Was she sick with the flu, or was this morning sickness?

"Are you sure? I know a couple of doctors live in this building and I would think, in weather like this, that at least one of them would be stuck at home. Let me call the concierge desk."

"No, Tyler, please don't. I need to rest, that's all."

He turned the music on, choosing yet another soft jazz CD. It was lovely and soothing, and he sat across from her and browsed through the magazine he'd taken from her earlier. "You let me know if you need anything."

Laney nodded. Her head still thumped like a bass drum, but her stomach was settling. She felt drowsy and eventually, with the music, the warmth from the fire, and Tyler's humming, she drifted off to sleep.

When she woke, Laney found herself underneath the black furry afghan that Tyler had wrapped around her the first night. She turned to see if he was sitting across from her. Nope, the room was empty, silent and a little chilly. She noticed the fire had been turned off, and she shivered under the blanket wondering where Tyler was. She sat up slowly, thankful that her head had stopped aching and her stomach was calmer.

"Tyler?" she sat staring at the empty room waiting for him to return. She glanced over into the kitchen, it was empty, too. Why would he leave when he knew she wasn't well? Laney sighed, a thin veil of apprehension clouding her judgment.

He couldn't have gone far, she concluded. The power's gone out again, the elevators aren't working, the snow's still falling. He must be here somewhere, she decided, and he would probably walk into the room any minute. She tried to cast aside her uneasiness.

Laney wandered to the window, all she saw was a sheet of white. With the afghan draped around her shoulders she sat back down to wait. She couldn't sit still for long, though, and got up again and wandered around the room. Where was he? Why wasn't he coming in to check on her?

She glanced at her watch and noticed that she'd been asleep for nearly an hour. Lord, she thought, I hope he hasn't done something stupid like gone to find one of the doctors in the building, and gotten himself or both of them trapped in the elevator when the power went out.

Laney tried to fight the flood of fear racing within her, causing a lump in her throat. And the more she thought about Tyler being trapped and unable to help himself, the more alarmed she became.

That had to be it. That's why he's not here. He went for help and now I don't know what to do to rescue him! She raced into the bedroom and picked up the telephone, the line was dead. Tyler, where are you?

She tapped on the guest bedroom door, and when she didn't get any answer, she opened it slowly. The room, like all the others, was dark and empty.

No matter how hard she tried, thoughts of him trapped in the elevator sent waves of panic careening through her. A flood of unbearable thoughts raced through her mind, each one worse than the one before, and she couldn't sort them out fast enough to think clearly about any of them. What should she do? Who could she contact? How would she contact them? What floor were they trapped on? And what if the power came on and the elevator crashed to the bottom? He could be lying there! Dead!

"Laney!" she scolded herself. "Get a grip! He's probably gone to the roof for some fresh air," she whispered out loud, remembering what he'd told her the day before about finding tranquillity on the rooftop. She shivered again and wandered back to the sofa. She decided she'd try reading so she picked up the magazine she'd glanced through earlier (what the heck were bond ladders anyway?). But she just couldn't concentrate on the words, and immediately tossed it aside, which did little to settle her churning stomach and brittle nerves.

Laney closed her eyes and took a few deep breaths attempting to calmly and rationally consider the situation. Where was Tyler and why would he leave me alone, she thought, especially knowing I'm not well? I told him I didn't need a doctor. But, he also knew I was physically sick, so that means either he's gone for a doctor in spite of my wishes, or he's gone up to the roof to be on his own for a while, or he's lying dead at the bottom of the elevator shaft! Her eyes burst open in fear.

She shook her head and yanked the afghan more securely around her shoulders and began rocking back and forth, her fists tightly clenching the blanket, tears tumbling down her cheeks. Visions of Tyler lying on the elevator floor bleeding to death invaded her thoughts and there was nothing she could do to get rid of them. She could even see the dark red blood staining his black shirt.

This was all her fault. She was the reason he was dead! Because she'd been dumped by Ramone that night, because her car died on her, because she forgot to re-charge her phone! If only she hadn't accepted his offer to take her home. If only she hadn't gotten sick, he'd be here now, safe and alive. Instead he was dying and she didn't know how to help him! He was dying because all he wanted to do was help her! Dear lord, it was all her fault! Laney choked on a sob.

"Laney! What's wrong?"

She gasped as she saw Tyler walking towards her. She covered the distance in a flash and was in his arms sobbing, fear and panic instantly replaced by relief and joy. "Tyler, it's you! Oh Tyler... you're alive!" she managed to gasp between sobs. "I thought you...were never coming back...I thought you were...dead!!"

More than a little curious at her display of emotion, Tyler held her and tried to comfort her, a bewildered expression on his face. "Laney, what's the matter? Did you have a bad dream?" He rubbed her back and tried to calm her.

"No...it wasn't a dream, Tyler. I thought you...were dead!" Warm tears streamed down her cheeks, her body shook with sobs, her arms locked tightly around his neck.

He whispered softly. "I'm not dead, Laney. I'm right here."

She looked into his eyes, a faint smile appearing beneath the tears. "I'm so glad... you're here, Tyler. I'm so happy... you're not...dead."

"Me too." He brushed a strand of hair from her face. "Now, will you please tell me what this is all about? Let's sit down." He tried to guide her to the sofa, but she shook her head.

"No, Tyler...just hold me. Please," she begged, thrusting her arms further around his neck, tightening her grip, her head firmly pressed against his shoulder. "Hold me."

He did as she asked. He wrapped one hand firmly around her back, the other stroked her hair and her tears finally subsided. "Are you feeling better, Laney?"

"I thought you were dead! Where were you?"

"I was in my study catching up on some work. You were sleeping soundly, I didn't want to disturb you."

"You were in your study? All this time?"

"Uh huh. Why? Where did you think I was?"

"It doesn't matter now." She sniffled.

"Yes, it does. I want to hear this." This time she allowed him to take her to the sofa and smiled when he wrapped her again in the afghan that had fallen to the floor when she rushed into his arms.

As Tyler poured her a glass of brandy, Laney wiped away the last of her tears, reality slowly dawning on her. How ridiculous, she thought, I've made a complete and total ass of myself for thinking those absurd thoughts, and now he has overwhelming proof that I'm a certifiable lunatic!

"Sip this." Tyler handed her the glass and sat down beside her. "Now, tell me why you're so upset."

Laney felt the amber liquid warm her throat. She stared at the glass in her hand, reluctant to look at him. "It's nothing...it's over now. Can we please forget it?"

"No, we can't. I want to know what happened here. If it wasn't a bad dream, what was it?"

"I'm sorry, Tyler. I got a little carried away, that's all. Let's drop it."

He reached for her hand. "Laney, something dreadful happened and it scared the hell out of you. I want to know what it was. You must tell me. Please."

Laney was unable to find the right words. "I...um... had a bad dream. You were right, it was a bad dream."

Tyler smiled, lifted her chin up, and turned her face to his. Their eyes locked and he leaned over and placed a gentle, lingering kiss on her warm, tear-drenched lips. "Please don't lie to me, Laney. What made you think I was dead?"

She shivered and released a ponderous sigh, realizing she had no choice. She had to tell him the truth. "I woke up and you weren't here." She closed her eyes reliving the fright that catapulted her into a state of near hysteria.

"And?" Tyler squeezed her hand, trying to coax the words from her.

"And I noticed you'd put the afghan over me and I remember you asking me if I needed a doctor before I fell asleep. I thought maybe that's where you'd gone, to find a doctor because you said a few lived here." She paused to clear her thoughts, unwilling to reveal the absolute terror that she had felt.

"And then?"

She sipped the brandy. "And I wasn't thinking straight. I was worried because I didn't know where you were."

"You were worried about me?" Tyler asked, an eyebrow lifting.

"Uh huh. I was groggy from my nap and not feeling all that well and I guess I got carried away."

"Carried away with what, exactly?"

Laney frowned. She did not want him to know the series of events that led her to believe he was dead. "Well," she spoke slowly, knowing eventually he'd get the truth from her. "I thought you'd gone for a doctor."

"Yes, you said that." Tyler squeezed her hand again. "Did you think the doctor killed me?" he suggested.

"No, no. I thought the power had gone off while you were in the elevator bringing the doctor here," she corrected him.

"Oh. And?" Tyler was still puzzled.

"And, I know all kinds of horrible things can happen in elevators when the power goes off and..." Tears welled in her eyes again, and she bit her lip trying to keep them at bay. "I saw a movie once where some people were trapped in an elevator, and the power went off and when it came back on..." Her voice faltered.

Tyler moved closer and placed an arm securely around her shoulders. "It's all right, Laney. Tell me."

"They all died, Tyler! The elevator crashed to the bottom of the shaft and everybody died! I thought you'd died! And it was all my fault!" Her tears flowed again, the sobs shaking her so fiercely Tyler took the glass out of her hand before the brandy spilled. He placed it on the table then gathered her tightly in his arms.

"It's okay, Laney. I'm not dead. I'm here. I'm right here. I've been here all the time. It's my fault I left you alone and I'm sorry. Please don't cry." He caressed her tenderly.

"I'm so sorry," she sobbed. "I'm not usually such a blithering idiot."

Tyler smiled. "You're not a blithering idiot. You let your very creative imagination run away with you, that's all. It happens to all of us, especially when we're not feeling well. Actually, in a way, I'm flattered."

She wriggled out of his embrace and stared at him. "Flattered?" She sniffled.

"Yes. I mean I don't like to see you upset, but..." He smiled and brushed away a tear as it rolled down her cheek, "it's nice to know you missed me."

"You have a crazy person staying with you, Tyler. I'd understand if you asked me to leave."

"After what you've told me, I would never do that."

Laney frowned. "What do you mean? I don't understand."

"Something's happening here, Laney. I've sensed it for a while and I think you have, too. And now I have proof."

Her heart skipped a beat, knowing he wasn't talking about proof of her being a certifiable lunatic. "Proof of what? What are you saying, Tyler?" she whispered, her eyes unable to meet his.

"I'm telling you that something is happening between us."

Laney's head jerked up, her eyes wide. "Are you saying what I *think* you're saying, because if you are, there is *no way!*"

Tyler grinned. "You can't deny it, Laney. I've already seen the truth. You and I have connected." His lips brushed fleetingly across hers, then he moved closer and kissed her deeply.

Laney pulled back sharply, trying not to enjoy what she really wanted to enjoy. "This conversation is over," she announced, walking away, rubbing her arms in an effort to shake off his lasting touch.

"Laney, let's not fight about this. Why can't you admit that we're attracted to each other? And that's probably why we're constantly fighting. We're trying to fight our attraction." He came up behind her, turned her around and cupped her face in his hands. "Let's stop fighting it, Laney."

Laney strained to get air into her collapsing lungs. "Tyler..."

"Shhh." He pulled her closer and lowered his mouth to hers. Laney shivered as his tongue probed her warm softness. She felt the strength in his arms as they encircled her and she slowly let her arms slide around his shoulders, her fingers playing with the curls resting at the nape of his neck. His cologne stormed her senses, depositing itself into her memory bank forever, and Laney could feel Tyler's passion as he held her tightly. He gently withdrew from their kiss and pressed her head against his heart. "Let's dance," he whispered.

"There's no music."

Laney felt the warmth as his hand slid down her back and his other reached for hers. He softly kissed each of her fingers, then put her hand on his chest. She could feel the thunderous beating of his heart as he slowly swayed.

"We don't need music. Just each other." He pulled her closer and began humming that same familiar melody she'd come to know and love.

Laney closed her eyes deliciously absorbing each and every sensation flooding through her as he expertly led her around the room. The snow fell and Tyler hummed. They didn't need music. They didn't need anything except each other. No other experience in her entire life could compare to this magical feeling of complete loving surrender. Laney wished time would stop. Right here, right now. And she wished she wasn't falling in love with this man, but it was too late. This man, this dance, this moment in time would endure in her heart forever.

"Tyler?" she murmured.

"Hmmm?"

"I'm sorry I thought you were dead."

"No need to apologize."

"Some crazy things have been happening to me these last few days. Call it temporary insanity."

He smiled and looked into her lovely deep brown eyes. "Laney, don't even give it a second thought. I know these last few days have been very difficult and, let's say, challenging for you. An engagement breaking off is tough at any time, then having your car die during the worst snowstorm of the year, and having no choice except to stay with a complete stranger is not exactly calming or comforting. But you know what?"

"What?"

"I still like you."

Laney squeezed his hand, and lay her head on his strong, inviting chest. "I like you too, Fred."

Tyler grinned and pulled her closer. "Then let's dance, Ginger."

They continued their dance, swaying to Tyler's soft humming, Laney letting him take complete control. She gasped in surprise as he twirled her around, then smiled when she was returned to his welcoming arms. He stopped dancing and held her tightly yet tenderly. She could barely inhale.

"I need you, Laney," he murmured, placing tiny kisses in her hair. "I need to make love to you."

She trembled as his kisses moved onto her forehead and down her cheek.

"Now, Laney." He pressed his warm body solidly against hers, providing her with proof of his arousal. His fingers combed through her silky hair as his lips found hers again, an urgency adding a roughness to his passionate kisses.

Laney shuddered knowing it was impossible to quell the longing and desire she felt for this man. She pressed her hands on his chest, feeling warm taught muscles beneath the soft fabric of his shirt. With a force totally foreign to her, yet instinctively knowing it was right, her trembling fingers began unbuttoning it, all the while savouring his hot tongue in her mouth moving sensually and rhythmically. Her hands pushed it over his shoulders and she moaned softly as she felt his velvety bare skin covering firm muscles. She tugged the shirt loose from his jeans and Tyler released his hold on her momentarily to let it slide down his arms and onto the floor.

"You have an amazing chest," she whispered, her hands sliding over every inch of it, releasing his scent yet again.

He raised an eyebrow, then grasped the bottom of her sweater. "Not half as amazing as yours, I'll bet," he whispered, a devilish grin appearing on his lips. In one swift motion, he lifted the sweater over her head and tossed it aside. He stepped back and swallowed hard, then reached out his hand to caress her cheek. His fingers lightly grazed her skin, moving slowly down her neck and onto her shoulder, where he slid her bra strap down. He pulled her closer and traced the same path with his lips and tongue.

Laney turned her head slightly as he reached behind her to unhook her lacy bra. Her hands combed through his hair, and her lips kissed his cheek, his neck, and that warm and oh so soft spot behind his ear. As the bra fell from her breasts, his mouth took its place, placing an already swollen nipple between his lips, his warm

VICTORIA GRANT

tongue darting across it, his teeth nipping it, teasing it, electrifying her.

Laney's breath strained. She could feel the dampness between her legs and a throbbing ache in her thighs that ignited a hunger so fierce, she knew it wouldn't be extinguished until she had him inside her. Red hot flames of excitement scorched her skin, every muscle contracted, every nerve ending tingled. "Tyler —" She breathed.

He reluctantly pulled away from her and their eyes locked. Without a word, he picked her up in his arms and carried her into the bedroom and tenderly placed her on the bed, then lay down beside her and took her mouth again. Laney closed her eyes, willing him to remove the barriers that were still between them and her hands grappled impatiently with his belt buckle as Tyler's soft, wet kisses covered her neck, her shoulders, her breasts.

"Laney, sweetheart." he murmured, helping her to unfasten the belt. His breath came sharply as she slowly dragged the zipper down and rubbed her hand firmly against the black briefs covering his rigid arousal.

He disposed of her jeans and panties in an instant, and rapidly removed the last of his clothing while Laney waited for his arms to hold her again. The white furry blanket underneath her bare skin felt luxurious and sensual, and her heart skipped a thousand beats as he moved his naked body alongside hers. He was beautiful, strong, hot and hard. And she was already damp and ready for him.

Tyler smiled softly and took her face in his hands and kissed her hungrily. Sparks of anticipation sent her into a giddy euphoria as he leisurely explored her every curve from the tips of her toes to the warmth of her ear lobes with his lips, his tongue and his fingers. He sensuously massaged and stroked, gently nibbled and nuzzled, and she knew she'd explode if he didn't enter her soon.

Laney savoured his caresses as his hand slid along her thigh, then his fingers moved inside her, a sensation she'd never experienced before. They moved slowly and softly and she sighed, impulsively arching her back so she could achieve more pleasure from his touch. He responded to her desire and began to expertly bring her to her first climax.

Tyler kissed her deeply as they rolled over and over revelling in each other's bodies. Laney, now on top of him, reached down to massage his erection. Tyler's breathing became ragged as she rubbed the solid shaft, increasing the pressure with each stroke. He finally couldn't stand it any longer. He rolled them over so he was on top and he entered her slowly and completely. Laney again arched her body to meet his, pressing him deeper inside her, finally feeling the satisfaction of having him exactly where she needed him.

"God, Laney," he whispered into her hair. "You're incredible."

"Love me, Tyler." She kissed his shoulder and neck, and wrapped her legs around his back locking her ankles, pushing him even further into her warmth.

Their bodies moved together, slowly at first savouring every new sensation, Laney's fingertips danced delicately over his spine and shoulders, and her hands cupped his perfectly toned bottom and hips. His hands roamed boldly over her breasts, all the while their mouths fused together with frenzied desire.

A driving force catapulted them both into another dimension, touches amplified, tastes devoured, and each sensation became electrified. They moved as one, faster and faster until each nerve ending ignited, sending them both to the outer limits of sanity. A wave of ecstasy engulfed Laney, and then Tyler, until finally they were both floating on the highest, softest cloud in the sky.

Slowly, very slowly, Laney came back down to earth. Tyler's head was on her shoulder, she heard him breathing heavily and felt his heated, exhausted weight on her. As she tried to uncurl her toes and return her breathing to normal, she placed tiny kisses along his damp shoulder, all the while inhaling his luscious scent.

Tyler sighed with contentment, shifted slightly, and smiled. The feather-soft kiss he gave her took her breath away, she barely felt his touch on her lips. It was the most erotic kiss she'd ever been given. He moved away.

"Don't go," she whispered and impulsively reached out to pull him back.

"I'm not going anywhere, my love." He kissed her shoulder then turned over, taking her with him, and Laney lay her head on his chest, her fingertips playing with his mat of furry chest hair, their damp, naked bodies still entwined.

"Laney?" he whispered, one hand resting on the curve of her hip, the other stroking her hair.

"Hmmm?"

"I...uh...we...seem to have forgotten something."

She raised her head to look at him, a nervous laugh escaping her swollen lips. "It didn't feel like we forgot anything."

Tyler grinned. "I was so into the moment, I forgot to put a condom on." He cleared his throat. "I'm sorry. It won't happen again."

"Right. I forgot, too. Sorry."

"We should take precautions next time."

Her hands roamed over the broad expanse of his chest. "We will. But there's no need to worry."

They lay in heavenly silence a long time, holding each other close. Finally, Tyler stirred and Laney rolled off him and watched as he stood up and blew her a kiss. "Be right back," he whispered.

Laney watched his lovely bottom, muscular back, and sexy, powerful legs walk away as she moved into the warm spot their lovemaking had created and snuggled up in the furry blanket.

A minute later he reappeared with a bottle of white wine and two glasses. "Turns out Duncan knew something we didn't."

Laney sat up anchoring the blanket under her arms. She held the glasses, which he filled to the brim. After settling in bed with her, Tyler held up his glass. "What shall we toast to?"

"All your hidden talents? Which aren't hidden right now," she teased. "Or perhaps strangers in a snowstorm?"

"Strangers at the start, but not now." He held up his glass. "To strangers, and getting to know a certain stranger very well."

They tapped glasses and Laney took a sip of the cold wine. Tyler put the bottle on the night stand and she snuggled into him, resting her wine glass on his chest. He kissed her long blonde strands and Laney closed her eyes, totally content.

"This is so much nicer than dancing," he whispered.

As Laney was about to agree, she sneezed and the wine glass fell from her hand. Tyler cried out as the cold wine splattered all over his body and the sheets.

Laney broke out in laughter at the startled look on his face. She rescued the empty glass.

"What's so funny?" He stared at her.

"I'm sorry," she managed between giggles. "It was an accident."

Tyler caught her arm and pulled her on top of him, making sure her breasts and tummy got caught in the cold, sticky liquid. "An accident, eh? How do I know that?" He raised an eyebrow.

"You suspect an ulterior motive?" She laughed.

"How do I know you didn't do this on purpose?"

"Why would I do that?"

"It gives you a great excuse to lick it all off."

"Is that why you got me covered in it too?"

"Absolutely." He grinned wickedly.

"I have an idea. Why don't we have a long, hot soak? Bubbles optional."

"I have a better idea. Let's have a shower." He offered his hand and pulled her off the bed, then led her into the bathroom where he started the hot water. He kissed her again. Intense, possessive and molten-hot kisses covered her face, her shoulders, her breasts and stomach as the steam enveloped the room. Their insatiable hunger for each other stirred once more. Before they stepped beneath the pulsating water, Tyler held Laney so close she was sure she'd never inhale again. His kisses became urgent and demanding and they made love in the shower, Laney astounding herself at her daring, yet exhilarating show of feelings for this man. Emotions and sensations she had never even dreamt of before were becoming a reality for her and she took immense pleasure in the boundless ecstasy Tyler brought her.

After they had dried each other off, enjoying the sensuous softness of the fluffy black towels, they sat by the fire in bathrobes. Tyler poured them another glass of wine and Laney rested her head on his shoulder as she sipped it.

"Watch where you put that glass," he warned with a smile.

She looked up at him, grinning. "I'll be careful."

Tyler sighed. "Isn't this marvellous, Ginger? To be together here all alone, nothing to do except hold each other until the world ends."

"I want to stay here forever, Fred."

# Chapter 6

Laney spent the next few days in a wondrous world, a universe so foreign and unfamiliar to her, yet one so thoroughly enchanting she didn't want to leave. The electricity kept going on and off, but it was Tyler sending a current through Laney every time he touched her that was a constant source of fascination and exhilaration to her.

They danced to Tyler's humming, oblivious to the falling snow and the real world outside. They had long conversations about their past, their careers, their families, their goals, their hopes and dreams. They cuddled by the fire to read or do crossword puzzles. They took turns preparing meals, although without electricity for hours on end, they both became experts at making salads and sandwiches, and they finished the wine that Duncan knew they would enjoy. They also found fun and sexy ways to enjoy all the chocolate and the ice cream. They played a few card games, and Tyler pretended to be totally devastated, but only for a minute, when Laney beat him at strip poker. They shared showers and bubble baths, and made love to each other in breathtaking ways, and not once did they get into a shouting match.

There was never a moment when Laney questioned what she was doing. To her this was a welcome escape from her family, her responsibilities, her real and tumultuous world. However, a nagging thought lingered at the back of her mind. She knew sooner or later the magical spell would be broken and she would have to go home. Laney had no idea what would happen after that, after she shared her important news with her family, but right now she didn't care. For once she decided to live in the moment and enjoy all the things she and Tyler could share. And she prayed the snow would fall forever, because she knew when it stopped, the fantasy would end.

On the morning of day six, Laney awoke early. Something was different, and at first she didn't quite know what it was. Then she realized sunshine was streaming through the blinds, and she heard the noise of traffic. The city was coming back to life and that could mean only one thing — the storm was over.

She turned to Tyler, who was sleeping soundly on his stomach beside her, his arm sprawled possessively across her belly, his knee resting on her thigh. Laney lifted his arm gently and crawled out of bed, careful not to wake him. She looked out and saw the plows had come through the night piling the snow high along the sides of the streets, and people were digging their cars out and shovelling sidewalks, attempting a return to their normal activities.

The time she'd been dreading had finally arrived. Laney knew she must leave. This fantasy had lasted longer than she'd ever expected and she knew her time with Tyler was over.

Her stomach knotted as she began to think of what kind of reception she'd receive when she got home and what exactly she would say to her family. She didn't have a clue where to begin or what to tell them, she hoped something suitable would come to her to help her explain the engagement being called off, and that the news of her pregnancy wouldn't start World War III.

She dressed quietly as Tyler slept, then went into the study to call a cab. Laney thought about leaving a note for him but decided against it. Last night they had shared some very intimate thoughts and Laney wanted those to be the last things he would remember.

As she pulled on her coat and boots, she heard the bedroom door open. She turned to find Tyler tying the belt on her favourite red bath robe.

"Laney...?" His hand rubbed his beard stubble. "Where are you going? Why do you have your jacket on?"

"I have to go home, Tyler," she stated simply, a lump forming in her throat.

"You're leaving?" He frowned.

She nodded. "Yes. It's time I let you get back to your life."

"Shouldn't I be the judge of that?"

"A lot of things have happened to me in the last few days, Tyler, and I've got a lot of explaining to do to my family. I want to go home and get that over with so things can get back to the way they were."

"Things will never go back to the way they were, Laney." His gaze made her catch her breath.

She looked away and fastened her jacket. "I have to go."

"Why so soon?"

"The storm's over."

"So?"

"So, I have to leave."

"Laney, it's going to take a while before the city digs out and everything starts moving again. Is the power on?"

She nodded. "Yes, the phones are working. I've already called a taxi."

The tension that had lain dormant for days immediately surfaced. Tyler's face hardened and he walked to the window and stared out at the snow-covered city.

"I should go. My cab is probably waiting."

He turned around. "So that's it. You're leaving."

"Yes."

"So you don't give a rat's ass about how I feel or what I want?"

Laney turned on him. "That's not fair, Tyler. This is hard enough for me as it is!"

"Is it, Laney?" he growled. "Tell me, how hard can it possibly be to walk out on me, to try to sneak out without telling me, without even leaving me a note? Damned difficult, isn't it?" He paced around the room.

Laney headed for the door, and turned one last time to look at him. "I'm sorry, Tyler. I didn't want to wake you. And I didn't leave a note because..." her voice failed.

"Because...?"

She turned away, not wanting him to see her tears. How could she possibly tell him why she hadn't wanted it to end like this without sounding melodramatic? Within the span of two minutes all the caring and intimacy they had shared for three days disappeared, shattered into oblivion, never to appear again. No more sparks, no more flames, no more heat. In its place, choking, chilling, black smoke strangled her thoughts and senses. All that remained were the ashes - their original resentment and loathing of one another.

"I have to go." She reached for the door knob.

"I have to go, have a nice life? That's it? That's all I get?" he snapped. "Don't you think we have a few things to discuss before you waltz out of here?"

Laney's voice was a whisper. "No. I'm sorry, Tyler, there's nothing to say. I...I enjoyed our time together, but the fantasy is over. We both have to get back to reality." She opened the door.

"This has been a fantasy for you? An escape from your real life? Some fun while the snow fell, is that it? Nothing more?"

Laney winced. "You don't understand!"

"What don't I understand? The fantasy is over part, or the leaving me part?"

Laney clenched her fists. All she wanted to do was leave without causing more damage. "There are a lot of things you don't know about me, Tyler."

"Perhaps, but there are a lot of things I do know about you, Laney." His wickedly sexy grin returned for an instant. "Like how much you love bubble baths and chocolate, and how you lose control when I kiss you in certain places."

"I'm trying to be serious! My life is very complicated right now."

"Then why are you attempting to complicate it even more?" he demanded. "You can't walk away without talking to me about our future, Laney. God, after everything we've shared these past few days, you owe me at least that much."

She couldn't. She just couldn't tell him why she had to go. She shook her head, fighting the rising sobs again. "We haven't got a future, Tyler. I have to go, my cab is waiting."

With a sob stuck in her throat, Laney walked out and closed the door behind her.

# Chapter 7

Laney hesitated before inserting her key into the mansion's front door, knowing all her family were probably inside. She knew they would want a plausible explanation for where she'd been during the snowstorm although she still hadn't thought of one that would sound convincing.

She tossed her hair over her shoulder, took a deep breath and opened the door. Time to face the inevitable. The enormous white marble floored entrance hall, framed on each side by winding staircases, with a white concert grand piano at its centre, was silent and empty. Laney's eyes scanned all the doors around the hall to be sure no one was coming or going. All clear. Laney closed the front door quietly. Her boots clicked as she walked swiftly across the highly polished floor and she winced as the echo reverberated through the emptiness. She sprinted up the stairs.

"Alaina!" a sharp voice rang out. "Where in heaven's name have you been? You've had us all worried sick!"

Laney turned, not at all surprised to find her mother standing at the foot of the stairs. "Hello, Mother."

Genevieve Calderone smoothed her expensively coiffed white-blonde hair into place and swiftly climbed the stairs, lifting her long, black skirt out of her way as she did. Even when housebound, she always dressed as if she were ready to attend a gala celebration for the United Nations. She followed Laney into her bedroom.

"Are you well? Where have you been? Why did you not call us to tell us you were safe? What have you got to say for yourself, Alaina?"

Laney pulled off her jacket and boots and put them away, trying to decide if a lie or the truth would be best to tell her mother. "I tried to call..." she began feebly, "... but my cell died."

"Where were you? I had all your brothers out searching the streets for you and that new car of yours, and they couldn't find you! I was very nearly tempted to call the Chief of Police to get the entire Toronto force out to search for you!"

"I had car problems again, Mother. A Good Samaritan rescued me." She smiled slightly, pretty sure her mother wouldn't accept such a simple and truthful answer.

Eve Calderone scowled with disgust. "What nonsense, Alaina. Now, where were you?"

"Did I tell you Ramone and I are no longer engaged?" Changing the subject seemed the fastest way to end that particular discussion.

"What did you say? You and Ramone are not getting married?" She ran over to Laney and lifted her left hand.

She slapped it sharply when she noticed the engagement ring was gone.

"Whatever did you do to that wonderfully handsome and rich man? He was perfect for you!"

"He wasn't perfect, Mother. No man is." Tyler's kisses invaded her thoughts and she struggled to shake them free.

"What in heaven's name am I supposed to do with the fifty-five-piece orchestra we hired for your reception? Answer me that! Guests are flying in from all around the world to attend this wedding, and now you tell me there is no wedding? Honestly, Alaina, I swear you do these things to upset me! We'll discuss this at dinner. I want your father to hear this news."

Laney sat on her bed watching her mother shut the door behind her, relieved that the initial interrogation had been swift and relatively pain free. The news of her pregnancy she'd save for later, much later.

Finally, she thought, back in my own home, in my own room. Now feeling physically and emotionally exhausted, she wanted to lock her door and sleep the day away.

A knock on the door stirred Laney from her thoughts. "It's open."

Noel Calderone, the youngest of her four brothers walked in. He was an extremely handsome man of twenty-six whose athletic physique and beautiful smile kept him busy with the ladies, who all felt sure they would make the perfect Mrs. Noel Calderone.

"Lane! You're back!" He sat on the bed beside her and kissed her cheek. "Where have you been? You've been giving Mother fits!" he chuckled. "She didn't know whether to call the hospital, the police or the morgue. I don't think I've ever seen her this worried."

"You could've fooled me. It certainly didn't seem as though she was happy to see me."

"She is, Sis. Believe me. So, where were you?"

"It's a long story. Did she really have you guys out looking for me?"

"Yes, she demanded we search the entire city. I went three blocks, got rear-ended twice and nearly slid into a parked car or five, so I turned around and came home. Sorry, Sis, you are important and all, but the Porsche couldn't take it." He got up and stared out of the huge bay window.

Laney smiled. "It's okay, Noel. You wouldn't have found me anyway. Was Daddy worried?"

"He was. He kept telling Mother that she should wait for a call from you and that no news was good news. He was concerned, he just didn't want her to panic. Where've you been?"

"Noel, I really need a hot bath. Can we talk about this later?"

"Oh, sure, Laney. You don't look any worse for wear, so I'll tell the fam you survived your ordeal. See you later."

Noel closed the door behind him and Laney went into her bathroom. A hot, scented bath with lots of bubbles to soak in was what she needed right now. She had to get things straight and clear in her own mind before she began explaining the recent events to her family.

But what was there to get straight? The facts were already straight and clear. Number one: a few days ago, she found out she was pregnant, she had been ruthlessly dumped by her fiancé, and the snow began to fall. Number two: hours later, she had entered an incredible world where she danced in a stranger's arms and made powerful and passionate love to him. She laughed out loud, amused at what her mother's reaction would be if she knew what had actually happened to her daughter since she'd last seen her.

As she ran her bath water, she heard another knock at her door.

This time it was the eldest sibling, Stephen, who let himself in. Like Noel, he had his father's dark hair, blue eyes and handsome looks, and stood a couple of inches over six feet.

"Hi, Laney. Noel said you were home. How are you?"

"I'm okay, thanks, Stephen. What's new here?"

"Since you asked, Mother's been having a fit over you not calling, Dad is bored out of his mind because he can't get to the office and because Mother's driving him crazy telling him that you were lying frozen in a snow bank. Jamie and Charles, I've hardly seen. I think they've been camped out in their rooms. I did see them once in a while in the library. Noel's had, at last count, twenty-seven ladies call him in the past forty-eight hours asking if they can keep him warm, and I've been busy catching up on paperwork. Basically, the same old, dull routine. So, what happened to you?"

"Car trouble."

"Again?"

"Yes, again."

"So where have you been?" he sat in a chair by the window.

"It's not important."

Stephen grinned. "Where were you, Sis?"

"Does it matter? I'm fine." Laney went to turn the bath water off.

"Glad to hear it. But where did you stay for six days?"

"At a friends' place." She searched the cupboard for towels.

"Who? Mother called practically all your girlfriends and no one had seen you. She also called Ramone's place and got no answer." Stephen winked. "Find someone special to share the storm with, did you, Sis?"

Laney frowned. "What are you getting at?" She didn't appreciate his insinuation.

"I'm curious where you've been hiding out." He paused. "You know, during the snowstorm?" he prompted.

"The person who stopped to help me with my car let me stay at their home until the snow finally stopped."

"What did you think of Tyler's condo?"

The colour drained from Laney's face as fast as the towels she was holding dropped to the floor. "How do you —"

Stephen smiled knowingly. "Tyler Hammond."

"I don't know who you're talking about..." she denied miserably.

"Yeah, right. I took a call on the business line from him ten minutes ago. Seems Tyler's more than a little annoyed with you leaving like you did."

Laney sat on the edge of her bed to collect herself. "What did he say? How do you know him? Why did he call here?"

Stephen chuckled. "I've known Tyler for quite a while; he's a business associate. He called to make sure you got home safely."

"Well, I did. And if he calls again, I don't want to speak with him."

"Fine." Stephen headed for the door. "I'll tell everyone you were safely snowed in with a business colleague and they needn't have worried."

Laney caught his arm. "No, Stephen, please. Don't tell them anything. I don't want anyone to know who I was with."

"Why not?"

"It's a long, boring story. You wouldn't be interested."

"Try me."

"No! Not right now."

"Then when? You know you'll be hounded about this, Sis. You of all people should know this family is tenacious until we get what we want. And now that you're home, safe and sound, you're big news! You can be pretty sure tonight's dinner conversation won't be about federal politics or the state of the economy."

"I need some time, that's all." Laney tried to explain. "Please, Stephen, don't say anything until I've had the chance to sort a few things out, okay?"

Stephen leaned over and kissed her cheek. "Okay, Sis, our secret. See you later." He shut the door behind him finally leaving Laney alone.

Damn Tyler, she thought, as she climbed into the tub. Why did he have to call here to check up on her? Could she not have one secret all to herself? Why did her entire family always have to know every little detail of her private life? Could they not be content with getting on with their own lives and leaving her in peace? Karma was always so happy to find new ways to make her life miserable.

Laney kept her soak brief, knowing if she didn't get downstairs fast, Stephen would drop hints to the rest of the family and before long, they would all know who she had spent the past few days with.

She dressed hastily, pulling on her favourite pair of comfy black leggings and matching oversized hoody. She heard the telephone ring. She listened at her door hoping Tyler hadn't somehow gained access to the family's private number. A sigh of relief escaped her as her mother was called to the phone.

Laney went down the rear staircase to the kitchen to find food. She hadn't eaten anything today and her stomach was snarling. She peeled a banana and nibbled it as she opened the fridge door and scrutinized its contents. She grabbed a yogurt cup and sat down at the counter to eat it slowly, delaying her return to the family as long as she could.

Finally, she decided she'd lingered long enough. Walking into the family room, or drawing room as it was called when entertaining guests, Laney was greeted by the sight of her entire family. Her mother was busy on the phone, her father's head was buried in a newspaper, and her brothers were either reading or on their cell phones.

"Ta-da!" Charles sang out, putting his book down. "Here she is. The long lost Calderone sister returns home to complete the perfect family picture." Charles, who had inherited his mother's blonde hair and brown eyes, and bore a striking resemblance to a young Robert Redford, got up and kissed his sister's cheek. "Welcome home. Can I get you a drink, Sis?"

"It's not even lunch time."

"Close enough. Glass of wine?"

Laney nodded. "Okay, thanks."

Boyd Calderone put his newspaper down and stood up to give his daughter a huge smile and a gentle hug. "Hello, Pumpkin." He kissed the top of her head. "It's nice to have you home. Are you okay?" When Laney smiled and nodded, he turned to his wife. "I told you she'd be home soon, Evey, and here she is, good as new."

Stephen winked at her. "Welcome home, Laney. Hope your time away from us was well spent."

She scowled at him, wondering how much Tyler had told him.

Charles handed her a glass of red wine. She took a few sips then sat beside Jamie on the sofa, enjoying the slight buzz the alcohol was beginning to have on her senses.

"So, Laney, tell us everything that happened to you these past few days." Noel said. "And don't leave out a thing."

Stephen laughed out loud. He seized a book and brought it up to his face to cover his widening smile. Laney's withering glance his way meant that further outbursts could prove fatal.

"There's nothing to tell. Ramone and I had dinner and we called off the engagement."

"You and Ramone are no longer 'Couple of the Year'?" Noel asked.

"We never were. The wedding's off."

Eve finished her telephone conversation. "What a horrible mess to put me through, Alaina. Do you know how many calls I'll have to make now to cancel all my bookings and arrangements for this wedding? My only daughter and all you do is give me grief!"

"At least you won't have to call the morgue, Mother," Stephen remarked.

"Really, Stephen. Don't be ghastly. I should think you'd be glad your sister is home in one piece. In this wicked weather, she could have been killed!"

"Yes, Mother." Stephen acknowledged. "We've all heard your 'Laney's frozen in a snow bank' story. My personal favourite is the multi-car collision. Yes, that full dismemberment insurance would've brought us a pretty penny." He faked a smile. "What do you think, Jamie, which was your favourite?"

Jamie tucked his shoulder-length blonde hair behind his ears and stroked his moustache and beard stubble. "I like Laney being held captive with one of Dad's fiercest corporate rivals," he chuckled, "and revealing all our company's secrets. Epic."

"Excellent. And you, Charles?" Stephen continued his game despite another warning glare from his sister.

"I like the stranger in the night theory. Much more romantic and elusive, wouldn't you agree, Laney?"

Laney's lips tightened as her gaze shifted again to Stephen. How much had he already told them? What did they know? She got up and poured herself another glass of wine. "I think you're all crazy. And to annoy you even more, I'm not going to tell you anything."

"Come on, Sis." Noel said. "Fess up."

"All you need to know is that Ramone and I are no longer engaged, so you won't have to worry about seeing the wedding photos plastered all over the internet and society pages of the newspapers with you wearing those horrid tuxedos he'd chosen. You should all be thanking me for that!"

"Why did you finally dump him, Lane? I thought you were going to go through with this 'merger' for the company's sake."

Jamie's remark caught Laney by surprise. "I...I didn't dump him, Jamie. I should have, though, a long time ago. He was the one who ended it. He decided we weren't right for each other. And I agreed."

Boyd had been watching his daughter. "No wedding, Pumpkin?"

"That's right, Daddy. Ramone and I called it off. I'm sorry, it probably means Ramone's father won't let you buy his company now."

"Nonsense. I'll have a chat with Carlos as soon as I can get through this white stuff and back to the office to review the merger documents. I'll convince him that even though our children won't be united, it's no reason our companies shouldn't be."

"What a true romantic you are, Dad." Charles laughed. "Aren't you the least bit concerned about Laney's state of mind over this news? She's definitely not the same gal who left here a few days ago, are you Laney?"

Again, Laney glanced at Stephen, who was pretending to be engrossed in the newspaper his father had set down. She shook her head slowly. "No, Charles. You're right. I feel quite different."

"You look different, too, Sis." Stephen folded the newspaper. "Doesn't she everyone? Don't you think Laney looks different?"

"Would you please stop worrying about me! I'm fine!" Laney cried. "I'm just fine and I don't want to talk about it anymore!"

"Oh, lighten up, Lane!" Jamie said. "Do you know how boring it's been here the last few days? All our hockey games were cancelled. I couldn't even get to the gym!" He looked over at Boyd. "Dad, we really have to start thinking about converting half of the basement into a home gym." He turned back to his sister. "You coming home alive with big news of a broken engagement is epic, Sis!"

"Well, I don't like being the topic of your conversation, dear brother." She got up quickly before another round of questions began. "I'll see you all later."

Up in her room again Laney was exhausted and sleep finally consumed her. Visions of Tyler swept through her dreams, which were disturbing and disjointed, nothing made sense or fit together. She woke up with a start, a cold sweat beading on her forehead. She sat up slowly, thinking about how much wine she had foolishly consumed on an empty stomach. Perhaps that's what was causing her chaotic dreams, or perhaps it was her pregnancy, news she had yet to share with the family.

She freshened up a bit, then caught up on her laundry while she sorted through her emails, both personal and business, which kept her busy most of the afternoon. The next time she checked her watch, Laney realized it would soon be time for dinner, and although not looking forward to her brothers' constant badgering, she had no choice but to face them again at the dinner table. Never had any family member been allowed to eat in the privacy of their own room unless they were sick. Dinner, her parents had always told them, was a family function and everyone must be present.

Laney made her way to the dining room, her stomach churning. She sat in her usual chair and nibbled on a dinner roll. Within a few minutes, the rest of the family joined her.

"Glad to see you could join us tonight, Alaina." Eve patted her shoulder then sat down.

"This is more like it!" Boyd smiled at her. "There's nothing I like more than having the entire family together for dinner. We missed you these past few nights, Pumpkin."

Laney smiled. "Thank you, Daddy."

"Ah, but did she miss us?" Stephen enquired, a mischievous grin lifting the corners of his mouth. "Or was her Good Samaritan so charming and wonderful she didn't have a chance to miss us?"

Having sat beside Stephen for nearly every meal since she was three, Laney's elbow found the pit of his stomach with unerring accuracy.

Charles heard Stephen's gasp. "What's going on over there?"

"Stephen has once again put his big foot into his even bigger mouth." Laney smiled sweetly. "I'm sure if he'd like to get through dinner without any more bruises, he'll measure his words more carefully."

Dinner was finally served and Laney hoped eating would shut Stephen up and reduce the conversation around the table. She piled her plate high with deliciously tender roast beef, creamy mashed potatoes, carrots and peas, and covered them all with thick, rich gravy.

"Hungry, Laney?" Noel noticed the quantity of food on her plate was much more than usual.

"Perhaps she had better things to do than eat while she was away, Noel." Stephen remarked casually. Laney shot him another fierce glare.

"Alaina, you haven't told us who you stayed with. I called all your girlfriends and none of them knew where you were."

"I wasn't with a girlfriend, Mother."

"Where did you stay?"

"Does it matter? I'm here now and I'm fine." She wished they would all drop the subject.

"I'm sure Mother would like to send your Good Samaritan a thank you card for taking care of her daughter," Stephen suggested.

"You haven't told us why your engagement was called off, Pumpkin," her father said.

"We weren't right for each other, Daddy. I thought everyone could see that." Laney suddenly didn't feel well. Perspiration gathered on her forehead and the back of her neck, nausea gripped her gut, and her head began to throb.

"Nonsense, dear," Eve said. "We honestly thought you two loved each other, didn't we, Boyd?"

Her father threw his wife a quick glance, then poured himself another glass of wine.

The food Laney ate was doing little to make her feel better. She tried to chew a bite of roast beef but couldn't even taste it. A million hammers pounded on her skull and she climbed out of her chair, leaning heavily on Stephen's shoulder as she did.

"Excuse me. I...I'm not feeling well."

"Laney? Do you need help?" Charles asked.

They all watched as she shook off Charles' inquiry and left the room. She used all her strength to climb the stairs and reach her bedroom, then lay on the cool satin quilt. Thoughts of Ramone and Tyler whizzed through her mind making her even dizzier.

Minutes later, a quiet knock on the door sounded and Stephen walked in.

"Lane?" he whispered. "Are you all right?"

As she answered, her stomach heaved and she rushed to the bathroom, her hand over her mouth. A few minutes later she emerged with a damp facecloth on her forehead and sat on the edge of the bed.

"What's going on, Laney? It's time you levelled with me."

"I don't know what you're talking about. Go finish your dinner."

"Not until you tell me what's happening."

"I have the flu or something. I'll be fine tomorrow."

"This isn't the flu."

"Maybe I'm sick of listening to you all get on my case."

"Bull. I have never known you to shrink from any of our infamous dinner discussions, Laney. You usually have the last word. So what is it?

Laney's stomach lurched again. "I can't tell you, Stephen. Not right now."

"Maybe I can help."

"No. I need time alone to think everything through."

"I'm not leaving until you tell me."

"Stephen, please leave. Let me figure things out for myself first."

"Are you sure?"

"Positive."

He hesitated. "Okay, Sis. If you need me, I'm here for you, you know that. Anytime."

Laney smiled. "I know. Thanks."

Once Stephen had closed the door behind him, tears overwhelmed her and she buried her face in the pillow. Ridiculous, she thought, still not believing the truth of the situation herself.

The door opened again and Stephen rushed to her side. "God, Laney, what is it? Please tell me what's wrong. I can't stand to see you like this."

He held her while she wept, trying to speak soothing words yet not knowing what the right words were. Laney shuddered and wiped her eyes.

"Tell me what's going on, Laney. Please."

Laney's tear-filled eyes looked directly into his. "I'm pregnant," she whispered.

Stephen stared at her. "You don't know that for sure, Lane." He smiled gently and rubbed her back. "You only spent a few days with Tyler; you can't be sure of anything yet. It's way too soon to know."

She shook her head. "No, no. Tyler's not the father. It's Ramone's. That's why I met him for dinner the night the storm began. So I could tell him about the baby." A new wave of tears engulfed her and she tried to talk between gasps for air. "But he doesn't want me...or our baby!"

Stephen wished this could be happening to someone else, anyone except his little sister. "Does anyone else know?"

"No. Oh, please, Stephen, you mustn't tell anyone. Swear to me you won't tell a soul."

"I swear. Our secret. What are you going to do?"

"I need to sort out a few things. Then I'll make plans and tell everyone."

"Laney, you're a very capable and intelligent woman. Why can't you raise the baby without Ramone? We're all here to help you. We'd make great uncles!"

"I know," she smiled. "I thought of that, but —"

"But what? Why can't you be a single mother?"

"Stephen, you know that's not even an option. Not with our old fashioned and conservative mother. She would literally kill me before she allowed a child to be born out of wedlock in this family. In fact, just telling her this news will be risky."

He looked at her. "There's something else you're not telling me, isn't there?"

Laney wiped away the last of her tears. "It doesn't matter."

"Yes, it does. What is it?"

Laney shook her head, unable to speak.

"Tyler." Stephen guessed. "It's Tyler, isn't it?"

Laney sighed. "I know it's crazy, he's a total stranger, but the time I spent with him was so incredible. I can't stop thinking about him."

"Does he know about the baby?"

"No." She panicked. "And promise me you won't tell him, Stephen, please. It's not fair to dump my problems on him especially since he doesn't really care for me."

"I wouldn't say that, Lane. He sounded genuinely concerned when he called to find out if you'd made it home safely. I know he's a decent guy and I'm sure you could talk to him about this. I can't say what his reaction would be, but I really think you two should talk. I got the impression you left his place with one or two matters unresolved."

"Stephen, please. Don't get involved. This is my problem and I'll figure things out for myself. Tyler doesn't love me and in time I'm sure I'll forget him. We had a brief fling and I fell head over heels probably because of how cruel Ramone was to me when I told him I was pregnant. It was amazing to be with a man who seemed to care about me, not the Calderone millions. But it was a fantasy world Tyler and I shared. And it's over now."

Stephen hugged Laney, nearly crushing her ribs. "Okay, Sis. Your secret is safe with me. Whatever you decide, I'll support you. Keep in mind, though, no secret stays a secret for very long in this family. You can't hide behind your bedroom door or your figure indefinitely. You'll have to make decisions regarding the baby and Tyler very soon."

"I know."

"Anytime you want to talk, I'm here. I'll tell everyone you've got the flu. It'll give you a few days to think about things and make your decisions."

"Thanks, Stephen. I appreciate that." She kissed his cheek. "You'll be the first to know."

Stephen closed the door behind him. Laney knew he would keep her secret, he'd always been the brother she trusted with important information, probably because he was the eldest. She loved all her brothers, very much, and they were all extremely protective of their baby sister. But Stephen had always been there for her, ever since Laney could remember, making sure their three brothers didn't tease or torment her too much with their silly jokes and childish pranks.

Laney knew there would be time later to tell her brothers and parents about her situation, for now she felt she needed to keep this news as close to her as she could, for as long as she could.

# Chapter 8

The next week Laney tried to get back into her old routine, especially at Calderone Industries. Her usual workload matched any of her brothers, each of them was a vice president of a specific section of the company. Laney's strength of purpose and stubborn streak had compelled Boyd to give her the job of Vice President of New Business Development, where she focused on the South American market, which always seemed to excel in fibre optic technology. She travelled to the region regularly, and Laney enjoyed the challenges and strategies presented to her on a daily basis, and she had proven she could handle the VP job as well as her brothers.

Unfortunately, her mother did not see it quite like that, insisting that once Laney was married, she would have to give up her career to become a full-time wife and mother. In her mother's archaic opinion, the business world would always be a man's world and Laney shouldn't get too comfortable because she was only visiting.

Her days lately consisted of surfing the internet, playing Solitaire, flipping through unanswered emails, and wishing she could confide in someone other than Stephen. He had been terrific, but she really would like another woman's point of view. Laney had lots of girlfriends, but felt she couldn't trust any of them with a secret of this magnitude. And she certainly could not tell her mother, not yet. Their relationship had always been tenuous at best and she feared this news would slash through what slender strand of love they did have for each other.

Her feelings about Ramone were never in dispute. She did not love him; she never had. She was twenty when they were formally introduced by the two families, everyone telling them what a perfect couple they made. Laney had been naively brainwashed into believing Ramone was the one man who could make her happy; however, she'd known for a long while that it was utterly untrue.

Her mother tirelessly assisted Ramone in getting closer to Laney and she never gave much thought to why high school and university chums, and her brother's friends and teammates had rarely asked her out on a date. She found out, too late, that her mother took great pleasure in squelching each and every one of the would-be suitors' efforts.

Her feelings for Tyler, on the other hand, were cyclonic. She had fallen for him, hard, but knew her feelings were based on a fantasy. They would probably never see each other again. Their time together had been glorious, even though it had been make believe. They'd been stranded together, trapped with only each other to look at and talk to for endless days and nights. Even the worst of enemies, Laney concluded, could learn to get along if forced to be alone together for that length of time.

Tyler had turned to Laney as a distraction from the problems with his divorce and his business. He had needed someone to take his mind off his troubles. And Laney happened to be that someone. It didn't mean anything.

She knew he would think the same of her, with her engagement breaking off and getting stranded in a snowstorm with a useless car, she would be in need of a little TLC. And he had given her that and more. His arms so tenderly enfolding her, his kisses so soft and sensual, Laney smiled remembering how wonderful it felt to be in his arms, never wanting to leave his warm embrace.

There had been moments during their time together when she had been very close to telling him she was pregnant, only something always stopped her. What it was that prevented her from sharing her secret, she wasn't entirely sure. Perhaps embarrassment or guilt. And no matter how much she tried to deny it, she knew she was falling in love with Tyler, and she convinced herself that her chance to be with him would be ruined if he discovered this news.

Whatever the reason, she sat today staring out of her office window at the gently falling snow when Stephen knocked and walked in.

"Lane! Great news! We finally closed the DeSantis Group buy-out. Seems Ramone's dad wasn't too upset over your broken engagement, and Dad and the Board members signed the final paperwork a few minutes ago."

Laney continued to watch the flakes gather on the shrubbery.

"Laney, did you hear me?" Stephen swung her chair around to face him. "Did you hear what I said?

"Stephen." She squinted at him, trying to focus on his face. "What are you doing here?"

"I told you, if you'd stop daydreaming long enough to listen to me. We finished the deal with the DeSantis Group."

"Oh. How nice."

"Carlos DeSantis is here right now and wants to see you. He's in the boardroom with Dad. You should go and say hello to him."

Laney's lips pulled tight. "My ex-fiancé's father is here to say hello to me. And what do I say to him, Stephen? Hello, Papa, get ready to become a grandfather?"

"Be civil, Laney. Please. I don't think he knows about your pregnancy. He wants to see how you are."

"Well, I'm not very well, am I? I'm pregnant! And his hopeless, low life son is the father of this baby and he bailed out! How am I supposed to be civil to him, Stephen?"

"Okay, okay, forget it. I'll tell him you're busy on a conference call or something. See you later."

Stephen closed her office door and Laney returned her gaze to the window, her thoughts drifting again to memories of a rooftop snowball fight.

Her phone buzzed, startling her. It was her new assistant. "Can you take a call, Miss Calderone?"

"Becky, please call me Laney. Who is it?"

"A gentleman. He wouldn't give his name."

"Okay, thanks, Becky. I'll be leaving after this so no more calls today."

"Goodnight, Miss Calderone, uh, sorry, Laney."

Laney was hoping it wouldn't be Luis Ramirez calling to discuss the new Venezuelan venture. The emails regarding this significant project had been sitting in her inbox, unopened, for days. She pushed the button to put the call on speaker phone. "Alaina Calderone."

"Ah, so you do answer the occasional telephone call - but only if you don't know who it is." The familiar voice of Tyler Hammond filled her office, sending shock waves up her spine. He'd left a number of messages on her cell. Laney hadn't bothered to call him back. What could she possibly say? He'd also sent a few emails to her business address, which she'd deleted without opening.

"Tyler." Laney tried not to let emotion enter her voice.

"You do remember! I'm honoured! I thought you'd forgotten all about me, as you haven't returned any of my calls or emails."

Laney drummed her fingers on her desk. Now was not a good time. There would never be a good time. "I'm very busy. What do you want?" she snapped.

"Not having a good day, sweetheart?"

"I am not your sweetheart, and my day is none of your concern." Laney sighed. "I assume you have a *real* reason for calling?"

"Let's have dinner tonight."

"I'm busy."

"Cancel."

"Not possible."

"Laney, we need to talk."

"We have nothing to discuss."

"I think we do. Should I drop by and see you then? At your office? Perhaps I'll bump into your father and I can tell him all about the marvellous time we had together during the storm. I'm sure he'd be interested to know who his daughter was with, don't you?"

A wave of panic engulfed her, so she decided to call his bluff. "Don't waste your time. I've already told my family who you are and where I was."

"Don't lie to me, Laney. Stephen tells me you're keeping our tryst a secret."

"That's blackmail!"

"Dinner. Tonight. Eight o'clock. My place. I assume you'll know how to find it. Oh, and I've stocked up on candles — just for you."

Laney punched the off button and the room went silent. She glared at the phone and whispered, "I'm not going to play these silly games with you, Mr. Hammond! Do us both a favour and leave me alone!"

He was toying with her, she knew that. How could it be anything else? He hated her from the minute he laid eyes on her! Why was he bothering her? Couldn't he let the past stay in the past?

Without warning, a sharp pain suddenly tore through her gut. She wasn't sure what it was, though she had felt this pain before. It seemed to happen every time she got angry or upset. Taking deep breaths and closing her eyes, Laney tried to think of something other than Tyler Hammond. Eventually the pain subsided. Great, she thought, now on top of everything else, karma is giving me an ulcer!

It was after seven when Laney got home. She had gone shopping after leaving the office, needing some time alone before facing the inevitable interrogation from her mother, who still could not believe the fact that Laney didn't have enough sense to marry Ramone.

She had absolutely no intention of going to Tyler's for dinner. She had to have time to sort out her problems, one of which he was fast becoming if he continued to threaten her with revealing their secret to her family.

Shortly after Laney arrived home, the family sat down to dinner. Stephen droned on about the DeSantis buy-out and Laney tried to stay interested by rearranging the food on her plate.

"Not hungry, Sis?" Jamie asked, pouring himself another glass of wine.

"Not really." Laney sipped her ice water.

"Did I tell you about the party we're hosting?" Stephen said in between bites.

"What party is this?" Eve asked.

"Mother, you know it's a Calderone tradition to throw a party when we've acquired another asset. We're going to invite all DeSantis Group employees here for our traditional Welcome Aboard party."

Laney nearly choked. "*What?* Ramone and his family are coming *here*?" she was incredulous. "After all that's happened?"

"Don't have a fit, Lane. According to his father, Ramone's flying south for a month's holiday. We'll have it while he's away."

"If we're going to have one of our famous parties, I'd better get started planning it as soon as we've finished dinner." The mind of Eve Calderone was never at rest.

Hours later, when Laney was getting ready for bed, Stephen knocked on her door.

"Laney, Tyler called me today," he said as he came into the room and shut the door.

"He called me, too."

"That's great! You two are finally talking."

"No, we're not. He invited me to dinner tonight with the threat that he'd tell Dad our secret if I didn't show."

"And you didn't show, so what now?"

"To be perfectly honest, Stephen, I'm beyond caring. I'm tired of being manipulated by the men in my life and I couldn't care less what he says or does. Besides, I've not been feeling too well."

"What's wrong?"

"Morning sickness. Not a lot of fun, especially when it hits morning, noon and night."

"Can't Doctor O'Brien give you anything for it?"

"I haven't seen him yet."

Stephen stared at his sister. "You haven't been to the doctor yet?"

"No."

"Laney, what the hell are you waiting for? For God's sake, you have to make an appointment to see him! How far along are you, anyway?"

Laney shrugged. "I'm not exactly sure."

"Promise me you'll get to the doctor. This week if possible."

"Okay, okay, I'll call him tomorrow."

"Is there anything I can do for you?"

"No. Thanks, Stephen."

"Goodnight, Laney."

Stephen was closing the door when Laney called him back. "You said Tyler called you today."

"He did."

"Well, what did he say?"

"We just talked."

"About me?"

"Yes, amongst other things."

Laney frowned. "You didn't tell him I was pregnant, did you?"

"No, I didn't. I told him to forget all about you and have an affair with Sarah."

"Who's Sarah?"

"My new admin assistant."

"How thoughtful of you, Stephen. Why are you trying to sabotage this relationship before it even has a chance?"

Stephen laughed. "I'm not doing that, Laney, you are. You said so yourself, you're tired of him and you want him to leave you alone. I don't think you really know what you want, do you? It must be all those pregnancy hormones making you stupid."

"Well, thanks very much!"

"Be honest with him, Sis. Tell Tyler about the baby. He deserves to know."

# Chapter 9

The Venezuelan project filled Laney's calendar now. She finally started working with Luis and found time to lend a hand with the planning for the DeSantis Party. Although not looking forward to the actual evening, she enjoyed the party preparation as it helped take her mind off her uncertain future.

Laney finally made an appointment with Dr. O'Brien, the Calderone family doctor, whom she swore to secrecy, above and beyond the usual doctor-patient confidentiality, because she knew her mother, once she found out, would employ a myriad of ways to extract any and all information she could from him about her daughter's pregnancy.

He estimated she was six or seven weeks into her pregnancy and gave her a prescription for a new drug that he assured her would ease the morning sickness without harming the baby. Laney found it helped to some extent, but she still had bouts of nausea on occasion.

It had been weeks since Tyler's dinner invitation. She was ambivalent about the fact that he had not tried to contact her again. It drove her crazy trying to figure out why this man pursued her persistently, and then backed off completely without a word. And he had not followed through on his blackmail threat, so, Laney thought, that's one problem solved. Not having Tyler in the picture to complicate matters would make her decision easier. Whenever she reached a decision.

The day of the party finally arrived and Laney stayed home from work to help with the last-minute details. As Christmas was just around the corner, the huge entrance hall was festively decorated and would be put to use as a dance floor later in the evening. Several ten and eleven foot fully lit Christmas trees stood beside the front doors and throughout the main floor of the house, and bright red poinsettias sat on every step of both staircases. The party planners her mother hired were busy stringing up the fresh pine and cedar garland on the stairs while the band set up at the center of the balcony overlooking the hall. A team of caterers busied themselves in the kitchen preparing the evening's banquet.

After a quick bite of lunch, Laney grabbed a few fresh strawberries from the kitchen, which she enjoyed as she checked her emails to be sure nothing urgent had cropped up. She relaxed for a while in a scented bubble bath, then, wrapped in her bathrobe, she explored her massive closet, sorting through all her evening gowns. This was a tuxedo affair for the men but knowing which gown was right for what occasion always frustrated Laney. She chose a favourite full-length, red sequined form-fitting strapless gown, which had a slit in the skirt that reached her thigh.

She swore under her breath as she tried to zip up the dress, exasperated that her figure was already losing its slender edge, and she fought with the zipper until it fastened. Was it pregnancy pounds showing up already? Or was it all that stress eating she'd been doing? She had eaten lots more chocolate than usual recently, thinking it would give her courage to share the news of her pregnancy with the rest of the family, which, naturally, it had failed miserably at. The dress was definitely tight but as she planned to have it on for only a few short hours, she decided she could endure the pinch.

She slid the matching sparkly combs into her upswept hair, then stepped into the red sequined heels, not looking forward to how sore her feet would no doubt be by the end of the evening. Ah well, she sighed, do it for The Family.

Laney finished applying her lipstick and took a final look in the full-length mirror. She never thought of herself as beautiful; she rarely bothered to look in a mirror at all, never liking what she thought was a long face, run-of-the-mill brown eyes and no outstanding features. 'Plain Jane' her brothers had always called her. Tonight, though, she looked different, perhaps even lovely. Maybe there was something in that glow all expectant women were supposed to enjoy.

As she went downstairs, she met up with Jamie, Charles and Noel, all looking dapper in their designer tuxedos. Charles held out his arm to escort her into the library for another Calderone tradition: the customary family toast before any of the guests arrived.

Stephen let out a whistle as she walked into the room. "Sis, you look great!"

"Thanks. I'll pass on the wine, if you don't mind," she said as Noel offered her a glass.

"And miss the toast, Pumpkin?" Boyd asked.

Stephen and Laney exchanged glances, both knowing she shouldn't be drinking any alcohol in her condition.

"Ice water?" Stephen suggested. "Doesn't matter what she toasts with, does it?"

The water was brought to Laney, who was sitting by the fire and a toast to the new acquisition was made. The family members scattered leaving Laney alone with her mother.

"I do wish Ramone was going to be here tonight, don't you Alaina?"

"No, Mother. I'm glad he won't be."

"Perhaps I'll telephone him. I need to speak with him regarding this engagement being called off. Such a silly thing you've both done."

"I wouldn't bother. There are sure to be lots of young, single, beautiful women here tonight. Why don't you concentrate on getting Charles or Jamie married off?"

"Charles and James, as well as Stephen and Noel, are far too young to think about marriage. It's your marital status I'm worried about. We don't want Boyd Calderone's only daughter to be an old maid, do we?"

"Mother, I'm not even twenty-five yet, for heaven's sake!" Laney got up and gazed out of the large bay window. The snow was delicately falling on the stately pine trees and shrubbery, and blanketing the limousines and taxis as they dropped off their passengers. She wished she could find something that would silence her mother as effectively.

"I'm off to the kitchen," Eve announced. "If I don't keep my eye on the caterers, God knows what they'd get up to! Now smile, Alaina, and go and greet our first guests."

Watching her mother leave, Laney said a silent prayer that she would not be the same kind of insufferable, overbearing mother to her own child.

She put the worrying thoughts of the baby out of her mind and went to the entrance hall to put in what she hoped would be a very brief appearance. Stephen and Charles introduced her to each guest and later, after doing her part to welcome the new employees, Laney chatted with Ramone's secretary, LuAnn, relieved to hear the confirmation that Ramone had indeed flown to Barbados three days ago and would not be attending tonight's festivities.

Once all the guests had arrived, Boyd Calderone stood on the balcony overlooking everyone gathered in the hall below. He signalled the band to stop playing and began his welcoming speech to the new employees of CI.

Laney had heard the speech so often she could say it in her sleep. She took the opportunity to rest her already sore feet and discreetly slipped away from the crowd into the empty library, where she poured herself another glass of ice water. She turned the lights off so the blaze from the fireplace and a few scented candles were all that lit the cozy room.

She sat down and pushed off her shoes, breathing an intense sigh of relief. She had forgotten how exhausting these parties could be and she glanced at the antique carriage clock on the mantle wondering how much longer these strangers would be in her home.

Ten minutes later, as she got up to leave, there was a faint knock on the door and Laney watched as Stephen walked in.

"Laney, there you are. Feeling okay?"

"I'm fine, Stephen. Has Daddy finished his speech?"

"Yes. Laney, we've had a late arrival, someone I want you to meet."

Laney's gasp caught in her throat as she looked up to see Tyler Hammond walk in. He looked perfect in his black tuxedo, not a hair out of place, a slight smile on his lips. His red satin cummerbund and matching bow tie glistened in the firelight, his eyes sparkling brightly as they caught and held hers.

Laney's mouth went dry, her lips tightened. She couldn't look away from his handsome face no matter how hard she tried. Sparks shot from the fire, danced on her sequined gown, then exploded around the room like fireworks.

"Laney, Tyler." Stephen smiled at his sister. "I believe you two know each other. I'll see you both later." He winked at Laney and closed the door behind him.

Tyler silently poured himself a drink while Laney struggled to get one tight high heel shoe back on her foot. "What are you doing here?"

"It's a party, isn't it?"

"You weren't invited."

"On the contrary, Stephen extended an invitation to me." Tyler walked past her slowly to stand at the fireplace.

Perfect. Big brother, also known as karma, strikes again.

"And," he continued, the familiar scent of his cologne refuelling her memories, "even though you stood me up for dinner, I didn't think it would be polite to do the same to you and your family."

"Please leave." Laney headed for the door, but he caught her arm.

"Not this time, you don't. I let you walk away once without answers and I'm not going to let that happen again."

She turned to face him, their lips a breath apart. "Let go of me, Tyler."

He smiled. "Can't. I just can't seem to do that, Laney, no matter how hard I try. Thoughts of you consume my days and invade my dreams, so I had to come here tonight to prove to myself, once and for all, that you're not worthy of my time or efforts. That you really are a spoilt, conniving little bitch, and I should forget you forever."

Laney's free hand swung around and slapped his face hard. "Get out."

Tyler laughed, placing his glass on the mantle. "Nice try, but you aren't that bitch, are you? You're acting like one so I won't get too close. And I want to know why."

Without warning he cupped her face in his hands and kissed her hungrily. Laney tasted the alcohol on his lips and sensed that wondrous feeling she had experienced for those few days which now seemed like eons ago.

He gently released her. "We have to talk." He guided her to the red velvet settee, where he pulled her down beside him.

"I have nothing to say to you, Tyler. Please leave."

"I'm not going anywhere until you answer my questions."

They both sat in silence for a long while, Laney staring into the fire, Tyler watching her closely.

"What questions?" she finally asked, her voice barely a whisper.

"For starters, why did you leave my place so suddenly before we had a chance to talk about our future? Why didn't you return any of my calls or emails, or come to dinner? Why are you going out of your way to avoid me, Laney? Did I turn into the plague?"

"I have to get back to the party. Goodnight." This time Laney was able to get away from him and she headed for the door.

"Damn it, Laney!" he yelled, darting after her. "What is it going to take to get some answers from you?"

Tyler followed her into the entrance hall where guests were dancing and chatting. He watched as she latched onto her brother's arm and pulled him into a dance.

"Laney!" Jamie was surprised to find his sister in front of him. "Care to dance?"

"Shut up and lead," she told him, trying to find Tyler who had disappeared into the crowd of guests.

"You dance divinely, Sis. I guess all those dollars Dad spent on your dance lessons weren't wasted after all." he teased.

"Jamie." Laney stared up at him. "Shut up." Her eyes scanned the room. There were so many men in black tuxedos it would be a miracle if she were able to spot him.

"Avoiding someone, are we?" Jamie asked. "Who are you looking for?"

"You don't need to know." Laney twirled in his arms. "Keep dancing."

"Okay," he shrugged. "But how can I protect and defend if you won't tell me who I'm protecting and defending against?"

Laney glared at him.

"I know," he nodded. "Shut up and dance."

She spotted Tyler chatting with Stephen, Charles, and a few others. He was in complete control of every situation, talking so easily with people he had never met before.

Jamie spun Laney around the floor and she lost sight of him again. The dance was nearly over now. One more spin and she could exit quickly and gracefully. She guided Jamie towards the nearest staircase.

"Say goodnight for me, will you Jamie?"

"Leaving so soon?" From out of nowhere, Tyler appeared behind Jamie, who he tapped on the shoulder. "May I cut in?"

Jamie smiled when he saw the look of acute irritation on his sister's face as he stepped aside. "Certainly."

Tyler took Laney into his arms and pulled her close. The music changed to that unforgettable jazz melody she knew so well, and out of the corner of her eye she noticed Stephen on the balcony with the band leader, a devilish grin on his face. Up to his old tricks again.

"You look ravishing tonight, Ginger." Tyler whispered in her ear. "Did I ever tell you red is my favourite colour?"

Laney tried to move to the rhythm except her feet would not obey. She felt clumsy and self-conscious dancing with Tyler with so many people watching, especially her family.

"You feel a little tense, my love. Relax and enjoy."

She closed her eyes wishing she could walk away, but that wasn't going to happen. Tyler held her tight and guided her effortlessly around the floor. The mesmerizing scent of his cologne reverberated through her senses and she surprised herself when she realized she was smiling. The Tyler Trap, she thought. You've gotten stuck in it again, you idiot!

With a deep sigh, she let herself surrender and leaned into him. He smiled and pulled her even closer. It didn't matter to her anymore who saw them, who noticed they were so close; she didn't care.

As she floated around the hall Laney became immersed in her surroundings. The Christmas tree lights twinkling, the distant chatter and laughter of the guests, the captivating tune, and the wonderful feel of this man in her arms.

Laney wanted to freeze time again. This man, this music, this moment. She rested her chin on his shoulder and let him take complete control. They moved as one, oblivious to every eye on them as they soared in the clouds, leaving all the other guests back on Earth.

Laney tried desperately to analyze her feelings for this man. There was no denying he had irresistible charm. And his powerful allure that paralyzed her every time she was near him was something she couldn't comprehend. But that magnetism was too powerful. It scared her. It had been fear that had kept her from returning his calls and meeting him for dinner. But, she asked herself, why fear such pleasure? No one made her as happy as he did, being held in his arms, dancing with him, making love to him. Nothing made sense any more. All she knew at this moment was she never wanted this dance to end.

Eventually the music stopped. And like before, the spell was broken. Laney stepped back forcing Tyler to release his hold on her.

"Goodnight, Mr. Hammond. Thank you for the dance." She turned and sped away before he could notice her cheeks had gotten as red as her dress.

"Not so fast, Ginger." Tyler managed to catch her hand. "We need to talk."

"Alaina, won't you introduce me to your divine dance partner?" Eve had intercepted Laney before she reached the stairs.

Karma just couldn't take the night off, could it? Laney smiled her best false smile. All right then, what harm would a very quick introduction do?

"Mother, this is Tyler Hammond. Tyler, this is my mother, Genevieve Calderone."

"Call me Eve," she gushed as Tyler kissed her hand.

"A pleasure, Eve." He smiled. "Such a lovely evening."

"Why, thank you. Tell me, what do you do at DeSantis?"

"Absolutely nothing."

Eve stared at him blankly.

Laney smiled. Seeing her mother speechless was indeed a first. "He doesn't work at DeSantis, Mother. And he has to leave."

"No, no, you mustn't go so soon, Mr. Hammond. You must tell me where you learned to dance like that. I saw you expertly twirling my daughter around the floor, you know!" She laughed as she wagged an accusing finger at him.

"He has a red-eye flight to catch, Mother, and he's running late for it." Laney knew she must act fast to thwart any attempt by her mother to get to know Tyler. "He has to go. Now."

"Now, Laney, my love, let's not be rude. I'd very much like to have a chat with you, Eve. May I get you a glass of champagne?"

"Certainly...'my love'? You called my daughter 'my love'? Alaina, is there something you'd like to tell me?" Eve studied her daughter's face.

Tyler smiled innocently as Laney's cheek colour deepened again to echo that of her dress. "No, Mother. He's an old friend, that's all." She glared at Tyler. "An old friend who has to leave *now* to catch his flight!"

"Tell me, Mr. Hammond, how long have you known my daughter? She's never mentioned your name before."

"That's not surprising, Eve, you see, Laney exaggerates a bit. We're not really old friends. I met her during that terrible snowstorm last month."

Eve's stare intensified. "How interesting. How did you happen to meet Alaina, Mr. Hammond?"

Laney bit her lip, racking her brain to think of something she could say or do to stop this inquisition before Tyler divulged too much. He had that devilish grin on his face and she knew he was enjoying every second of her predicament.

"Let me explain—" Laney began.

"No, let me." Tyler interrupted.

"Mother!" Laney's voice climbed, "isn't that Daddy over there? I think he's looking for you."

Eve turned. "Yes, Boyd does seem to be searching for me. Do stay, Mr. Hammond, I'd like to continue this very interesting conversation later. Excuse me." She gave Laney one long glare before moving through the guests, smiling and gushing as she did.

Tyler grinned. "Nice save."

"Get out."

Laney headed for the sanctuary of the library, with Tyler close on her heels. He shut the door behind them and pointed a finger at Laney, who was staring into the fire.

"Enough running, Miss Calderone. It's time you were honest with me. Now what the devil is going on in that brain of yours?"

Laney spun around, fighting sudden tears. "What do you want from me, Tyler? Why won't you leave me alone?"

His silent stare bore holes in her heart and she turned away unable to endure the pain. The dying embers crackled in the fireplace.

"We really don't know each other, Tyler." Laney said after a long while, turning to face him. "Those days we spent together were magical and wonderful, but they were so very different from who we really are. It was a fantasy; can't you see that?"

A deep scowl darkened his face. "Is that what you think it was?"

Laney threw up her arms. "Oh, of course it was! Only an idiot would think what we experienced for those few snowy days could be anything like real life! We're not in the middle of a Fred and Ginger movie now, Tyler. This is real life, not a fairy tale, and it very rarely, if ever, has a happy ending!"

"You have to work at it, Laney. Real life can have a happy ending."

"Not this time, not for us."

"Why not?"

"It's not possible."

"Come and sit down so we can talk."

"Why can't you accept what I've said and let it end?"

"Because that's not what I want. And I'm damned sure that's not what you want either!" Tyler's eyes locked onto hers and he moved closer and took her hand. "Laney, please, you have to tell me what's going on. Have you gotten back with your ex-fiancé?"

"No."

"What then?"

"Nothing."

"Bullshit! What is going on?" Tyler struggled to maintain his temper.

"It's nothing, damn you!" Laney pulled her hand away.

"It must be something! You can't stand there after that dance we shared and tell me there's nothing between us!"

"Tyler, please —"

"Tell me!" his voice ripped with emotion.

"It's none of your business!" Laney yelled.

"Did she tell you she's pregnant?"

Laney turned in horror to find Ramone standing in the doorway, a pompous grin on his lips. "Ramone..." she gasped. "What are you doing here?"

"I heard about this little deal our folks made and I came back to get in on the fun! Who's this clown?" He pointed to Tyler who was staring at Laney.

"Is this true, Laney?" Tyler whispered.

Her nightmare had become a reality. Laney slumped on the couch, wishing the flames from the fire would devour her.

"How long have you been standing there?" she asked, ignoring Tyler's question.

"Long enough." Ramone smirked.

"Get out." Laney whispered. "Both of you, leave me alone."

Ramone, his slicked back hair gleaming in the firelight, laughed and poured himself a drink.

"Is this true, Laney?" Tyler repeated, standing directly in front of her.

"Is what true?"

Tyler's voice rose again. "I'm not in the mood for games, Laney. Are you pregnant?"

Their eyes locked. After an extremely raw silence, she looked away and whispered, "Yes."

Tyler stepped back, his face refusing to betray his emotions. Then he strode out of the room, closing the heavy door behind him.

Laney stared into the dying embers. So now he knew. And the news had produced the precise reaction she knew it would. It had ended before it had begun, this relationship. Why bother dreaming when all she ever got were nightmares? There was a good reason she hated fairy tales. Prince Charming didn't exist in her world. She wiped warm tears from her cheeks. Karma must really despise her.

Minutes later, she heard Ramone helping himself to yet another drink. She thought he'd left but he sauntered over and stood in front of her. "You look great tonight."

"Get out."

"What kind of greeting is that for your fiancé?"

"You're not my fiancé any more, remember?"

He pulled a familiar ring out of his pocket and tossed it into her lap. "Put this on."

She watched it fall, not touching it. "Go to hell."

"Why Alaina, I'm shocked! Such language!"

She glared at him. "Why did you have to come here tonight? Haven't you done enough to ruin my life?"

"I told you, I want to marry you."

"After our last conversation, what makes you think that's ever going to happen?"

Ramone reached for her hand, she snatched it back.

"Alaina, my dearest, I want what's best for you and our baby."

Laney laughed. "Since when? The last time I saw you, you went crazy when I told you I was pregnant with your child. You said the most cruel and hurtful things to me, Ramone, and I will never wear this ring again! I will never be your wife!"

The door opened and Stephen barged in. "Laney," he began, "I saw Tyler leaving. What happened?" He spotted Ramone. "What are you doing here?"

"Stephen." Ramone shook his hand. "Nice to see you again. Congratulations on your new acquisition."

"Thanks. I thought you were out of the country."

"Papa called me with all the details, so I came back to ensure everything is legal and on the level."

"I'm sure you'll find all the details to be in order. Both teams of lawyers have already said the purchase is as good as done."

Laney got up, the ring dropped to the floor. "I have a headache. Goodnight."

"Laney, wait. What's going on with Tyler?" Stephen asked.

She paused at the door. "Ramone was more than happy to break the news of my pregnancy to him." She turned to Ramone. "Thanks again, for your impeccable timing."

Stephen grabbed Ramone's tuxedo lapel, protective of his sister's fragile state of mind. "What did you say to him?"

Ramone shrugged his shoulders, trying to release Stephen's grip. "I told the guy she was pregnant. Thought he should know."

"When I thought the time was right to tell him, I should've been the one to do it. Ramone strikes again!" Laney's sarcastic laugh filled the room. "I honestly don't know why I bother with men."

# Chapter 10

The morning after the party, Laney woke up late and was the only person at the breakfast table. Judging by what little food was left on the buffet, she knew most of the family had already eaten and she was thankful for the time alone. As she enjoyed her second cup of tea, her mother entered the room and sat in her customary place at the end of the table.

"Good morning, Alaina."

"Morning, Mother."

"Last night was an excellent party, wouldn't you agree?" She poured herself a cup of tea.

Laney nodded. "It was lovely."

"I noticed your Mr. Hammond left before we had a chance to finish our chat. Why was that?"

"He probably went to catch his flight, Mother, and he's not *my* Mr. Hammond."

"Is that who you stayed with during the snowstorm last month?"

"Does it matter?"

"It might." She added 3 teaspoons of sugar to her tea. "I saw Ramone last night."

Laney concentrated on her banana muffin, unwilling to enter today's combat zone.

"Awfully decent of him to cut his holiday short to return to you, wasn't it?"

"He didn't return because of me, Mother."

"That's not what I understand." Her teaspoon clicked loudly as she stirred the hot liquid.

"What *do* you understand?" Laney hated herself for asking.

"Ramone and I had a nice little chat."

Laney sipped her tea, dreading the next few minutes, hours, days, weeks...

"And your wedding will be going ahead as planned."

"*What*?" Laney stared at her mother in disbelief. "You can't be serious! I told you he and I are no longer engaged. No engagement, no wedding."

"There will be a wedding, Alaina. You and Ramone will be married as planned. He'll be dropping by later today to put that ring back on your finger where it belongs."

"I don't want his ring and I certainly don't want *him*! Surely you haven't forgotten, Mother, Ramone was the one to break off our engagement."

"Yes, you told us that. However, you conveniently forgot to tell us a very significant piece of information, didn't you, Alaina? The reason *why* Ramone broke off your engagement." Eve's voice was icy cold and Laney looked up to find her mother's wild eyes piercing through her. Her stomach plummeted to the floor and her heart shrivelled up, leaving her empty, desolate, and more alone than she'd ever felt. She remained silent.

"Seems there's the rather momentous news of you being with child. Is that right, Alaina?"

Laney slowly nodded. "Ramone told you."

"I suppose I should be grateful *somebody* told me! What were you planning to do with this baby, Alaina? Give birth in your room, then put the child up for adoption hoping your family wouldn't notice? Or were you planning to run off and elope with that Hammond fellow you were glued to last night on the dance floor?"

"I'm making plans, Mother. I was going to share them with the family tonight at dinner," she lied.

"Your plans are cancelled. You and Ramone will be married, as the invitation states, on February twentieth. We can have the seamstress alter your dress if you're showing by then."

It took a concentrated effort for Laney's trembling hands to place her teacup into its saucer without breaking either piece of fine china. "I am *not* marrying Ramone, Mother. I *hate* the man! You wanted me to marry him so CI could buy the DeSantis Group. And that's done, so there's no reason whatsoever why I should have to endure having that man as my husband!"

"I assume he's the father of this child? That alone is reason enough for the marriage," Eve's voice dropped from her usual acidic pitch to a very low, menacing tone. "Unless he's *not* the father of your baby."

Laney stared at her mother. "*What?!*"

"It wouldn't surprise me if you and Mr. Hammond have been intimate. He certainly danced with you like you were his to keep."

Laney's thoughts raced to find the right words that would stop this relentless invasion into her private life. "Tyler has nothing to do with this. Ramone is the father. But he doesn't want the child, Mother. Did he tell you that he hates children, that he never wants to be 'saddled with the responsibility of raising a kid'? Those were his own words! Did he tell you that?" Laney's voice had risen to a frenzied level, and it was all she could do to keep her breakfast down.

"And what about you, Alaina?" Eve's voice went up an octave. "Did you give *any* thought to the serious consequences your lovemaking could bring about? Did you even think to protect yourself from such a cataclysmic event? Or did you lead him on, teasing him, seducing him, so the man had no choice but to bed you?"

"Mother!"

"You listen to me, young lady. I will not have you embarrassing your father, his company, or this family by giving birth to a bastard child! Your father and I have worked too long and too hard in this city to have you ruin the Calderone name! You shall be married. And when the time comes, we'll have to announce that it was a premature birth."

Laney jumped up, spilling her tea. "That's all you *ever* care about, isn't it Mother?" she yelled. "Your precious reputation in this city! To hell with what your family needs! Things are only done around here if they're for the good of the company and the Calderone name! Well, to hell with the Calderone name, to hell with your reputation, and to hell with you, Mother!"

Stephen barged through the door nearly knocking Laney over. "What is going on in here? I could hear you both all the way upstairs!"

"A little disagreement, Stephen," Eve told him. "Nothing to concern you, dear. Please leave."

"He knows I'm pregnant, Mother." Laney tried to calm down as she wiped the tea off her leggings.

"I see. Your brother finds out before I do. How typical."

"Mother, let's discuss this like adults." Stephen recommended, gently propelling Laney back into her chair.

"There's nothing to discuss. Ramone will be here later to give Alaina the engagement ring, which she will accept, and the two will be married in the new year as originally planned."

Stephen smiled at Laney and patted her hand as she shook her head vigorously. "Mother, there's more than a few problems with that arrangement."

"There are no problems with that arrangement. The baby must have a name and a father. Ramone provides both."

"Ramone doesn't want to be a father. That's why he broke off the engagement in the first place. Laney doesn't love him, she never did. And let's be honest, Ramone doesn't love Laney, either. Why trap them *and* an innocent child in a loveless relationship?"

"He told me last night he wanted to marry Alaina."

"I don't believe you!" Laney shouted.

"We discussed the matter in detail and he finally agreed that the honourable thing to do would be to marry you."

Laney blinked back the tears. "No, he wouldn't say that! There's no way he would change his mind that quickly unless...unless —"

"Unless he was offered something in return." Stephen eyed his mother suspiciously. "Okay, Mother. What did you promise him if he'd marry Sis?"

Eve's face stiffened. "Really, Stephen. I don't know what you're talking about."

Stephen winked at Laney. As the first born, he had a certain advantage when dealing with their mother and she saw a tiny spark of hope. Things may not turn out all that bad with Stephen on her side.

"What's the deal, Mother?" he insisted.

"I refuse to answer such an uncivilized question."

"Mother, what did you offer Ramone to make him want to marry Laney, a woman he doesn't love, who's pregnant with his child, a child he doesn't want? I'm willing to bet it's something with a lot of zeros on it."

Eve sat back in her chair, fingering her ever-present triple strand pearl necklace and glared with contempt at her daughter and eldest son. "I have nothing more to say on this matter. The wedding will take place as originally planned. This discussion is over." She got up and walked out.

"*No!*" Laney cried. "I will *not* marry that man! I won't!"

"Laney, calm down."

"Oh God! Stephen, she's gotten her hooks into Ramone somehow! This is a nightmare!"

Stephen poured his sister another cup of tea. "The first thing you're going to do is calm down. Then you're going to stop worrying. It won't do you or the baby any good. Mother's hiding something and I intend to find out exactly what."

"How?"

"Leave it to me." He sat down across from Laney and poured himself a cup of coffee.

"I hate Ramone, Stephen, I really do. Because of his insufferable arrogance and selfishness, and because of the situation he's put me in. Sometimes I can hardly believe I'm in this mess!"

Stephen reached for a muffin, deep in thought. "What's the one thing Mother's most upset over?"

"Her standing in Toronto's social sphere."

"No, it's more than that. It goes deeper than that. Perhaps if we gave her a wedding she'd be quite happy."

Laney's eyes darted skyward. "Obviously! That's exactly what she wants. Ramone and I to get married!"

"Did I say Ramone?"

Laney stared at her brother.

"She wants the baby to have a father and a name, however, it doesn't necessarily have to be Ramone, does it?" Stephen smiled at his sister.

"You don't mean Tyler?"

"I do mean Tyler. He left here in quite a hurry last night, though I think I can persuade him to return. You'll have to do your part too, Sis."

"This isn't funny, Stephen! I don't want to see him anymore, and besides, now he knows I'm pregnant, he won't want anything more to do with me."

"Come on, Lane. You said yourself you're head over heels for him. And after seeing you two together on the dance floor last night, I'd say he's got it pretty bad for you, too."

"He stormed out without giving me a chance to explain!"

"He was in shock. Let's give him another chance."

"Let's not."

"Look, Laney, you don't have much of a choice. It's either Ramone or Tyler. You decide."

Stephen was right. Her choices were clearly limited.

"Stephen, you know I appreciate your help; however, there's one thing no one's considered yet."

"What?"

"Me. Why doesn't anyone listen to me? Doesn't what I want count for something? I mean, it is *my* life, isn't it?"

"Certainly. So, what do you want?"

"I want to be left alone. I want time to think."

Stephen got up, shaking his head. "Oh, Laney, for God's sake, will you *wake up*? All I've heard you say is you want time to think, you need time to be alone, you want to do what *you* want to do. But you *don't know* what you want to do! Months ago, you liked Ramone enough to marry him, now you hate him with a passion. Weeks ago, you told me you thought you were crazy in love with Tyler, now you can't stand the sight of him."

"Leave Tyler out of this."

"Fine, but it's time you accepted the fact that Ramone is not entirely to blame for this pregnancy! You have to take responsibility for fifty percent of the situation you're in now, and quite frankly, I think you should've been more cautious knowing how careless Ramone usually is!"

"Don't yell at me!"

He paced around the table. "Somebody's got to yell at you, Laney! Look at you! Pregnant for two months and no rational decision yet concerning your future! Do you want to have this baby? Or an abortion? Do you plan to deliver the baby, then give it up for adoption? Are you going to raise it yourself? These decisions need to be made, Laney, and now!"

He sat down again and reached for her hand. "I want to help you, Sis, except I can't do any more. I've covered for you at work and with the family. I had to practically beg you to see the doctor. I know you're overwhelmed by this, Laney, you're frozen with fear, but you've got to do *something*! When are you going to accept this situation you're in and *do* something for the health and welfare of both yourself and your unborn child?"

Stephen's words hit her like machine gun fire, blasting her mistakes, firing at her indecision, ripping apart her carelessness, shattering her with truths until Laney could listen no longer. First Ramone, then Tyler, then her mother, and now Stephen! Didn't anyone understand? She ran from the room, leaving Stephen shaking his head.

When Laney reached her room, she closed the door and sat by the window for a while deep in thought, watching the birds flutter around the feeders in the garden. Stephen had been right about one thing, she was frozen with fear. Did she want this baby? Would Tyler even consider being with her knowing she was carrying another man's child? Could she have the baby without being forced to marry Ramone? Could she be a single mother, knowing what her mother's demands were? Too many questions that had no answers and made her future so uncertain.

Laney wondered if asking for her father's assistance would make any difference. She had always been Daddy's Little Girl but even she knew her father would only go so far if it meant going against his wife's decision. The children had learned at an early age that Boyd ran the company, Eve ran the household, and this was definitely a domestic issue. There had been a few times in her life when Laney and her brothers had witnessed their father change their mother's mind on an important family issue, yet it was a rare occurrence. Even so, she had to try. She could not, in any way, picture herself as Mrs. Ramone DeSantis.

She knocked on Boyd's study door.

"Come in."

"Daddy?" she walked into the room and shut the door. "Do you have a few minutes?"

Boyd looked up from his desk and smiled at his daughter. "For you, Pumpkin, anytime. What's up?" He rose from his chair and invited Laney to sit on the sofa.

Laney perched on the edge of her seat. "Dad, I'm sorry if my...condition...has embarrassed the family. That's the last thing I want to do."

"You haven't embarrassed the family, Alaina. I know your mother is very distressed about your situation, but you haven't embarrassed us." He sat down beside her.

Laney nodded and tried to smile. "I didn't plan this."

"No one does." He smiled gently.

"I need your help, Dad. I don't want to be forced into marrying Ramone. I don't love him. I never did."

"How long have you known this?"

Laney shrugged. "I'm not sure, exactly. A while."

"Is there someone else?

Laney winced.

"I need to know the truth, Alaina. Be honest with me."

"Okay, I don't know what Stephen's told you —"

"Stephen hasn't told me anything."

"Oh. Well, I'm pretty sure I've fallen in love with another man. The Good Samaritan who helped me during the snowstorm."

"Does this man have a name? Do I know him?"

"Tyler Hammond. No, I don't think you know him."

"So, what do you want to do?"

Laney took a deep breath. "I think I'd like to have the baby and raise it with you and Mother's help, here in our home. And I definitely don't want to marry Ramone."

Boyd nodded and remained silent.

"And I know as soon as Mother hears this, she'll want to kick me out of the mansion, and will probably disown me! Daddy, I can't marry Ramone. I just can't! I'll be miserable for the rest of my life! I don't know if I have a future with Tyler, but I do know for certain my life won't be a happy one with Ramone." Laney tucked a strand of hair behind her ear.

Boyd took his daughter's hand. "I think I understand. You're asking me to perform the simple and straightforward miracle of changing your mother's mind, is that it?"

"You know what she's like, she's ruthless!"

"Preaching to the choir, Pumpkin." he grinned.

"Daddy, I need your help to convince her that I never loved Ramone and I don't want to marry him. I mean, this is my life, not hers, right? Why can't I do what I want with my life and my baby?"

"Alaina, my dearest, you know your mother always has her children's best interests in mind, she wants what she thinks is right for you. I admit sometimes her methods could use examining and fine-tuning, but she only does what she does because she loves you and your brothers."

"I know, Daddy —"

"I will guarantee you, right now, we would never disown you or kick you out of this house, no matter what happens. I can't see your mother ever being that angry with you. And even if she tried, I would put a stop to it. It will never happen."

Laney smiled and nodded.

"Now, as for trying to change her mind about this marriage, Alaina, I understand, and for what it's worth, I agree. You'd be a better mother on your own than you would be if you were to marry Ramone."

"Thank you, Daddy."

"What about Tyler? Do you think he'll want to be in a relationship with you, knowing you're carrying another man's child?"

Laney shook her head sadly. "He left rather abruptly when he found out I was pregnant."

"So, that means the man you love doesn't want to be with you, and the man you hate wants to marry you — all because of the baby."

"The reason Ramone wants to marry me now is because Mother promised him something, probably money. When I told him I was pregnant, he went crazy, he called off our engagement, said he never wanted kids. I know he really doesn't want me or this baby, all he wants is the money!"

Boyd nodded. "So my job is clear. I have to influence three people."

"If anyone can do it, Dad, it's you."

"Ah, buttering up the old man. Nice touch, Pumpkin." He grinned and winked at her. "Alaina, you're my only daughter and I've always wanted you to be happy, like I want all my sons to be happy, too. I can't promise what the end result will be, but I will talk to your mother. Convincing her won't happen overnight, though, keep that in mind."

"What should I do in the meantime?" Laney already knew what he was going to suggest.

"Don't upset your mother by attacking or challenging her on this. She'll be more receptive if you're not constantly demanding that she sees things your way."

Laney stood up, nodding. "Okay. Thank you, Daddy." She smiled at him.

Boyd got up and hugged his daughter. "Leave it with me, Pumpkin, and I'll do what I can."

"Thank you. I love you, Daddy."

"And I love you, Alaina."

Later as the family ate dinner, Laney sensed an uncomfortable tension flooding the room. There was not much conversation as everyone seemed to be busy with their own thoughts, which was definitely not normal for a family dinner.

Once or twice Laney caught Noel, Jamie and Charles watching her and knew at once why the atmosphere was so strained. She realized her mother had shared the news of her pregnancy and none of them knew what to say or do. She glanced at her mother hating the smug, superior smile on her face.

She also noticed Stephen was not at the table tonight, and when she asked why, her father told her he had to return to the office to take care of some urgent business.

That was a lie, she thought. Stephen never went near the office in the evening, especially on the weekend. She knew he had become tired of defending her. It was time to let her face the family on her own for a change.

"Eat up, Alaina. You need to eat healthy now that you're eating for two," Eve advised. "By the way, dear, did I tell you Ramone called earlier and he'll be dropping by later this evening. You will take the ring back and marry him, won't you, Alaina?"

It wasn't really a request. Laney knew it, her mother knew it, all the family knew it. What choice did she have right now?

"Alaina, did you hear me?"

She looked over at her father who smiled slightly and gave her a quick wink.

"Yes." She ignored her brother's stares.

"Excellent." Her mother smiled widely. "I'll call the seamstress in the morning and let her know we'll drop by for another fitting on your wedding gown soon. Now eat those vegetables, dear."

After dinner, Laney wandered into the dark library. The room was vacant, so she pulled a book off the shelf and sat by the fire, trying to take her mind off Ramone's impending visit. She heard the doorbell and seconds later Ramone entered the room with her mother.

"Laney, darling," he embraced her tightly. "I'm so glad you've reconsidered."

Laney recoiled from his touch as Eve scurried around the room turning on all the lights. "I'll leave you two alone now," she said. "I'll be booking your European honeymoon first thing in the morning!"

When she left, Ramone sat down beside Laney and tried to hold her hand, which she yanked away.

"So here we are again. I suppose I should apologize for the things I said to you. It's not *all* your fault you're pregnant." He took a tiny blue box out of his pocket and pulled the ring from it. It glittered wildly in the firelight. He tossed the ring in her lap. "Here, put it on."

After her conversation with her father, Laney decided she would have a back-up plan in place just in case. She stood up, the ring falling to the floor. "Ramone, let's get a few things straight right now." She stared at him. "This marriage will take place on one condition and one condition only."

"What one condition is this?"

She turned to face him. "You don't touch me. Ever again. You keep your hands, lips and everything else to yourself during this travesty of a marriage. I don't love you and I never will, so there will be no physical contact. I'm doing this so my child will have a name and a home. That's it. I hate you, Ramone."

Ramone picked up the ring, a malicious smile creased his lips. "Didn't work out with Hammond, I take it."

Laney frowned. "How do you know his name?"

"Put this on before Mamma comes back." He tossed the ring to her again, Laney let it fall again.

"Do you agree to the terms of this marriage?"

He got up. "And what if I don't? You have a luscious body, Laney. And you will have for a while until you get fatter. How am I going to keep my hands off you?"

"You'd better find a way, or you'll find yourself without everything you take for granted, including that neat little package my mother promised you."

"What neat little package?"

"I'm not a fool, Ramone. I know exactly what it was my mother offered you if you'd marry me. I'll have our family lawyer draw up a pre-nuptial agreement, which you will sign, stating that if you come near me with the intention of physical contact, I shall have all the things you so dearly love taken away from you. Do I make myself clear?"

"Perfectly."

"You agree to these terms?" Laney questioned him again, both surprised and disappointed to hear him agree so readily to her idea. She would have bet big money that he wouldn't stand for such madness and walk out, leaving her mother to run after him, begging him to reconsider.

"Sure, why not?" He moved closer, rubbing her forearm.

Laney frowned as she moved away from him. "Okay, good. I'm trusting you'll keep your word, Ramone."

"Who are you trying to kid? I've had you before and I'll have you again beyond our wedding night! Men like me are irresistible, and you'll have your hot little hands all over me before you know it!"

Laney was infuriated. "Get out, Ramone! Now!"

"Don't be hasty, darling. We haven't finished our transaction yet."

He pulled her to him and pressed his lips viciously against hers. Trapping her arms behind her, he pushed her up against the wall. She struggled to get away, which made him tighten his grasp, making it impossible for her to break free.

She felt his rough tongue invade her mouth and her stomach churned at the thought of what she must endure on their wedding night if her father was not successful. She was disgusted by his lack of gentleness and her thoughts ricocheted back to Tyler. Never had she been kissed, held, or loved as she had with him. He was a man who knew how to treat a woman.

Ramone finally released her and she slapped his face.

"Now, now, we're not married yet. I take it your little contract becomes valid *after* the vows are said?"

He was right. Oh lord, Laney prayed, help me get through the next few weeks.

Stephen came into the library and stopped when he realized the room wasn't empty. "Oh, sorry to intrude.

I came in to get the newspaper." He grabbed it off the desk and turned to leave.

"Stephen, have you heard the latest?" Ramone lit a cigarette.

"What's the latest?" He glanced at Laney, who had her back turned.

"Your dear sister and I are to be wed. Isn't that grand?"

"You're kidding, right?" Stephen fell into a chair opposite Ramone.

Laney turned around. "No, Stephen. He's not kidding. We're going ahead with the wedding. I've taken your advice to be responsible for my actions and try to give this baby a normal family life."

"Normal? Sure!" Ramone complained.

"I'm glad to see everything will work out for you both. Congratulations, Ramone. You're getting a great lady."

"Not really, Stephen. We'll be married you see, however your darling little sister has devised a wicked plan whereby if I get her, I lose."

Stephen turned to Laney. "What's he talking about?"

"He'll be signing a pre-nuptial agreement that will explicitly state no physical contact in the marriage."

"Are you nuts, Sis? No man would agree to that!"

Laney smiled. "He has."

"Why?"

"Because he knows if he doesn't cooperate, he'll lose all those dollars Mother promised him."

"Is this true, Ramone?"

"Could be." He shrugged his shoulders and flicked his cigarette into the cold fireplace.

"You two are crazy! What kind of toxic atmosphere is that to bring up a child?"

"The kind that no more children will come into! I refuse to bring another child into a home where the parents hate each other!"

"What about birth control, Laney?" Stephen got up. "There are lots of things available to make sure you don't get pregnant again."

"No! No way! I hate Ramone and refuse to be intimate with him ever again! I'm only marrying him because Mother is demanding I go through with it."

Stephen nodded. "The very best reason to get married."

His sarcasm was not lost on Ramone, who chuckled and picked the ring up off the carpet.

"Don't patronize me, Stephen. You made it perfectly clear this morning that I'd better make a decision and fast. Well, I have. What other choice is there?"

"What about Tyler?"

"What about Tyler? He's the one who walked away when he found out about the baby. And I haven't heard from him since. I can't force him to do anything he doesn't want to. What kind of relationship would that be?"

Ramone stood up. "The same kind you've trapped me in."

Laney looked at him, disgusted. "Are you still here?"

"Laney, you have to speak with Tyler before you go ahead with this." Stephen suggested, glancing at Ramone apologetically.

"There's nothing to talk to Tyler about. He made his decision when he walked away. Now I'm making mine."

"When I suggested making a decision, this isn't quite the one I thought you had in mind."

Laney shrugged.

"Okay, Laney. If you're willing to spend the rest of your life with this man, good luck." Stephen tucked the newspaper under his arm and left the room.

"So, you gonna put this rock on your finger?" Ramone asked, throwing it at her a third time.

Laney caught the ring and stared at it. It was a beautifully cut diamond solitaire, yet it meant nothing. A piece of jewellery. A sparkling stone on her finger. A rock glittering in the sunlight.

Ramone walked over to her and slid the ring on her finger. He kissed her cheek and whispered, "I know we'll both be very happy with this decision, Mrs. DeSantis."

Laney watched him saunter out of the room laughing, hating her life.

# Chapter 11

The next couple of weeks passed rather uneventfully for Laney. Her family had accepted the fact that she and Ramone would be married and her mother prattled on endlessly every chance she got about how this would be the wedding of the century and how lucky the baby was to be born into one of the richest families in the country.

Laney visited Dr. O'Brien again, getting more medication from him as her morning sickness had not eased off. He cautioned her that her blood pressure had risen a little, and she booked an appointment for her first ultrasound to be sure her pregnancy was progressing as it should.

The Venezuelan project was in high gear now, Laney was putting in extra hours to try to complete it before the new year. Due to her condition, her father had suggested the principals from Caracas come to Toronto instead of her travelling there, which they had done. However, a few unusual issues had arisen in her last meeting with Luis so Laney wanted to consult with Stephen about them before she had a conference call with Luis later in the day.

Laney knocked on Stephen's office door, she heard 'Come', and walked in. When she looked up from her file, she was stunned to find Tyler Hammond sitting in the chair opposite Stephen's desk. She stopped abruptly, all words in the English language abandoning her except one. "Tyler."

"Laney. I...ah... was just leaving." He got up, but Stephen motioned to him to sit down.

"Hi Laney. Have a seat. What brings you by?" Stephen smiled at her.

Tyler sat and watched Laney sit in the chair beside him.

"I'd like to discuss the Ramirez acquisition, Stephen, whenever you're ready," Laney glanced over at Tyler, "but this obviously isn't a good time." She stood up and headed for the door, unwilling to let Stephen take control of this irritating dilemma she now found herself in.

"No, stay, Laney. Please." Stephen said. "Tyler was telling me his plans for the holidays. What is it you're doing for Christmas, Tyler?"

Laney turned and hovered behind her chair, her fingers digging deep into the supple leather.

"I'll be out of town over the holidays," he answered.

Laney breathed a sigh of relief. "Where are you going?"

"Out of town."

"How nice. I hear it's quite warm there this time of year."

Stephen's telephone buzzed and he grabbed it. After a few seconds, he got up. "Must run. Charles needs my help. Back in ten." He dashed out of the office, leaving

Laney staring after him, her mouth wide. He had left her alone with Tyler *again!*

"How are you, Laney?" Tyler asked softly, allowing his eyes to wander down to her tummy.

"I'm fine, Tyler." Oh, great conversation this is, Laney mused.

"Laney, I owe you an apology."

She frowned. "You do?"

"Yes. I'm sorry I left your party in such a hurry. It was very rude of me, and I hope you'll forgive me."

"It's understandable, Tyler, given the circumstances. There's nothing to forgive."

"Yes, there is." Their eyes met and he smiled, sending a familiar tingle through her gut. "It's almost lunch time. Have you eaten?"

"No, not yet."

"Why don't we go and grab a bite and we can talk?"

Knowing it was useless to resist, she nodded. "Okay, let me get my coat and purse."

After a short ride in Tyler's BMW, which brought back bittersweet memories for Laney as she inhaled his soul stirring cologne, they sat in a nearby restaurant and ordered lunch.

"It's nice to see you again, Laney." Tyler's gaze lingered on her face. "You look fabulous."

"Thank you. I feel fine. A touch of morning sickness every now and again, and my blood pressure's a little high, but other than that, the doctor says I'm doing fine."

He smiled. "Laney, I want to tell you why I left your party in such a rush, and I hope you'll understand. You see, the main reason Tracy and I are divorcing is because of children."

"I didn't know you had any children, Tyler."

"I don't. We tried, naively thinking it would improve our relationship; however, we could never conceive. We were both tested and the fault, it was discovered, was mine. Tracy wanted a child desperately so she went looking for a man who would give her one."

Laney looked away, unable to cope with the pain on his face. "I'm sorry, Tyler. I didn't know."

"It's not information I usually share. No man likes to be told he's incapable of becoming a father, nevertheless, I had to accept there would be no children in my life."

Laney nodded.

"So you can imagine my shock when you told me you were pregnant."

Laney looked up and met his gaze. "I was an idiot not to tell you sooner."

"I want to make things right again between us, Laney. Maybe those few days we spent together during the snowstorm weren't complete reality, but I know what I felt. And I know you felt it, too. I want us to start again. I want to do what's right for you and our baby."

"*Our* baby?" Laney stared at him. Oh, dear lord, she thought, he doesn't know the baby's not his. "Tyler, before you go on —"

"Let me finish, Laney, please. For the first time ever, I realized I'll be responsible for more than myself in this world. Soon we'll have a tiny new-born depending on us for everything - formula and dry clothes, clean diapers and warm baths, and most importantly, loving parents.

I can't let you go through that alone. I know we got off to a rocky start, but we can work things out, I know we can. I want us to turn those amazing few days into a beautiful lifetime."

Tears welled in Laney's eyes as she gazed at him. What could she possibly say now that wouldn't make him hate the very sight of her for the rest of his life?

"Tyler..." she began, "there's something important I have to tell you."

His eyes never left hers. "Laney, things can work for us. No relationship is perfect, we both know that, and now we have the responsibility of a new life to think about. We should be making plans, starting now."

"Tyler, please. I must tell you something." Tears burned her eyes, blurring her vision.

"What is it, my love?"

"This baby —"

"What about our baby?"

"I'm sorry, Tyler. This baby isn't yours. Ramone is the father of my child."

Tyler collapsed back into the chair and blew out a long, agonizing breath. "Ramone? Your ex-fiancé is the baby's father?"

She nodded. "Yes. That's why he broke off the engagement, because he absolutely hates children. I thought you knew, I thought Stephen would've told you."

An emotion Laney guessed was betrayal sliced through his face, causing his jaw to clench and his eyes to narrow as he gazed at her unbelievably. "Nobody told me."

Tears trickled down her cheek. "I am so sorry, Tyler. I don't know what to say."

He glared at her ready to unleash his anger. "You're telling me that you made love to *me* while you were pregnant with another man's child?" His voice rose, then he looked away, his eyes darkening. He turned back, leaning into the table, his voice a harsh whisper. "That's why you weren't overly worried when we didn't use any protection, isn't it? I thought it was because you were using some form of birth control, but that wasn't it at all, was it? You weren't concerned about *getting* pregnant because you already *were*!"

Laney knew she deserved everything he was throwing at her, but she defended her position. "The day I met you was the day I found out about my pregnancy and told Ramone and he dumped me! I was in shock over what happened and I was trying to figure out what to do next! And, while I was trying to sort everything out, my car died and the worst snowstorm of the century hit — and you came along."

Tyler smirked. "Yes, I came along. How convenient."

"Look, I didn't ask to stay with you, did I? In fact, I did everything I could think of to leave your place! I knew I had some very important decisions to make even before you came into my life."

Tyler was silent, slowly turning the water glass on the table.

"I appreciate what you did for me. You were the shoulder I needed, I'll never forget that. It was a difficult time for me and you helped me through it."

"That's no excuse!" Tyler slammed down the glass, water droplets flying everywhere and dissolving into the white tablecloth. The blood vessels in his neck were ready to burst. "Your pregnancy is a vital piece of information, Laney! You don't keep that sort of thing a secret!" he shouted. "Why the *hell* didn't you tell me?"

Other restaurant patrons were now glancing over to see why the noise level at table eleven had risen above the acceptable norm.

She bit her lip. "I know you probably won't believe this, Tyler. There were times I came so close to telling you. Especially the day I thought you'd died in the elevator —"

"The first time we made love," he reminded her. "Without a condom," he added spitefully.

Laney looked away." Somehow I couldn't do it. So many things happened so fast, I was so confused and mixed up. I blame it on pregnancy hormones. I'm still not thinking straight."

"Perhaps you'd better start, my dear. Babies have a habit of needing their parents' complete attention, so I suggest you prepare yourself for the enormous responsibility that's ahead of you."

"I'm sorry if this ruined everything, Tyler."

"Turns out there's nothing to ruin, is there?" He grabbed her left hand. "I see by this ring your engaged again, right?"

Laney's mouth tightened as she jerked her hand out of his grasp. "That's none of your business."

"Damn you, it is my business! Do you love him?"

"No. If you must know, I hate him."

"Then why the hell are you marrying this man? A man you don't love, who surely doesn't care at all about you or the child?"

"I told you. He's the father."

"So?"

"So, he'll provide a home for me and a name for the baby."

"That's it?"

"That has to be enough."

Tyler sat back as the waiter arrived at their table and placed a glass of wine in front of him and refilled Laney's water glass.

Tyler sipped his wine. "So why the sudden change of heart on his part?"

"You don't need to know," Laney snapped.

Tyler's laugh was cruel. "Ah, the Calderones strike again! What a surprise! Anything that can be bought, the Calderones buy. Companies, politicians, yachts, a husband, doesn't matter. Tell me, what's the going rate for a husband these days? One who will prevent the only daughter from becoming a single mother and scandalizing high society?"

"How *dare* you!" Laney shouted, leaping to her feet. "How dare you say those things about my family!"

Tyler got up, too, so swiftly that he almost knocked over his chair. "Tell me when the momentous occasion takes place, so I can be out of town."

"February twentieth. You're not invited."

Tyler laughed scornfully. "Believe me, my dear Laney, even if I was, I certainly would not show up to watch you make a mockery of marriage." He pulled out his wallet and tossed some bills on the table. "I've lost my appetite," he growled, turned and swiftly left the restaurant.

Laney stared after him, her blood boiling. Who gave him the right to talk about her family like that? She wanted to run after him to set him straight on a thing or two, but her knees buckled and she fell into the chair. Dizziness overwhelmed her and nausea took control. She sipped her ice water and took deep breaths unsure of what was happening.

Was this the 'occasional discomfort' the doctor had told her to be ready for? Did this have anything to do with the baby or was it merely her body's way of reacting to Tyler's spiteful comments?

Laney managed to flag down the waiter and after cancelling their food order, asked him to call her a cab. It took all her strength to get out of the chair, and when the waiter noticed her distress, he called another waiter over to help who recognized Laney and wanted to call one of her brothers. Laney begged him not to. She didn't want them involved, they'd only send her to the doctor again.

By the time she got home, the nausea had subsided, though her head was still pounding furiously. She called Becky to tell her she wouldn't be returning to the office and asked her to reschedule the conference call with Luis.

Laney decided a nap would help soothe her frazzled nerves. She lay on her bed and closed her eyes, thoughts of Tyler and his words echoing in her mind. *"I want to do all I can for you and our baby..."* he had said. *"...we can work things out... I want us to turn those amazing few days into a beautiful lifetime..."*

Lord, she thought, why couldn't this baby be Tyler's? What singular force is at work here complicating my life? What evil fate is to blame for throwing me and Ramone together right before I was to meet this amazing man? Karma, again?

Her life with Ramone would be loveless and boring, she knew that. She would become, in essence, her mother. A new generation of the typical 'society wife' getting involved with charities, gala events and city politics to fill her days.

On the other hand, life with Tyler would be exciting and always changing. He was a man with captivating charm. Anything he wanted, Laney pondered, he'd be sure to get. Too bad he didn't want her anymore. She really hated karma.

# Chapter 12

"Laney, wake up, it's Christmas Eve!" Noel shouted as he banged on her bedroom door, then barged through. "Wakey, wakey, Sis!"

Laney groaned into her pillow. "Noel, if you want to live to see Christmas Day, get out now."

"Come on, Lane! It's Christmas Eve! And there's a gift here for you!" Noel smiled, knowing this would get her attention.

Laney propped herself up on her elbows. "A gift? Who from?" she asked, yawning.

"No idea. It arrived five minutes ago."

Laney sat up. "Okay, I'm awake. Where's my present?"

Noel went into the hall and reappeared with a huge box, which he deposited in her lap. Laney glanced at the address label on the package. "Dorman's!"

Noel let out a whistle. "Even I know Dorman's. It's *the* most elite women's fashion boutique in the city. Someone's laid down a lot of cash for whatever's in this box."

Laney tore at the wrap and gently lifted the lid. After removing layers and layers of fine gold tissue paper, she caught her breath. She sprang from the bed and lifted a black velvet ball gown from the box. It was exquisite. Beautifully designed with tiny diamonds surrounding the plunging V-neckline at the front and back of the dress, the sleeves billowed from the shoulder, then tightened at the elbow and came to a point, edged in more tiny diamonds, over the hand.

"Oh my. It's stunning," Laney whispered. "Who could've sent it?"

"Here's the card." Noel picked it up from the bottom of the box and handed it to her.

Laney read it out loud. "*'To my darling fiancé. Thought you'd need a new dress for tonight's party, as you're probably too fat to wear all your others. Ramone.'*"

"Ramone?" Noel repeated. "Ramone bought this? That's not like him, is it?"

"The gift, no. The romance and tenderness in his words, however, is typical." Disgusted, Laney ripped the card in half and tossed it in the waste basket. Yes, she'd put on a few pounds but she could still fit into most of her clothes. "How insulting." She picked up the dress again. "It's a beautiful gown though, isn't it, Noel?" She ran a gentle hand over the luxuriously soft velvet and fingered the tiny diamonds.

"You'll look gorgeous tonight." Noel smiled.

"No, I won't."

"Huh?"

"I'm not wearing this tonight."

"Why not?"

"Because I'm not! Ramone may enjoy telling all the other women he's been with what to do, but that's not happening with me! I had planned on wearing my white silk dress tonight."

"He won't be happy," Noel chuckled.

"Do you think I care? I refuse to be told what to do. I'm not wearing it."

"Suit yourself, Sis. See you later." Noel left shaking his head, convinced he'd never figure out male-female dynamics.

Laney hung the dress in her closet and tried to forget it while she showered. Why would he do such a thoughtful thing like buy her a magnificent gown, then ruin the moment with some poorly chosen, insensitive words?

As she climbed out of the shower, her cell rang.

"Darling, did you get my gift?"

"Ramone."

"Did you get the gift?" he repeated tersely.

"Yes. Thank you." It took all her self-control to be polite.

"Does it fit?" he asked. "If it's too small, I can have them send over a larger size before tonight."

Enraged, Laney nearly snapped her cell phone in half. "I can't wear it, Ramone. Awfully sorry, but I don't have any shoes to match this dress. I'll be wearing my white silk gown tonight, so please don't wear that ugly white tuxedo you own, or we'll clash." Laney clicked her phone off and strolled into the bathroom with a smile on her face.

During breakfast, another gift arrived. This time Stephen brought it into the dining room, where everyone was eating.

"It's for you, Laney." He handed it to her. "A little early, isn't it?"

"Another one?" Noel asked.

"What do you mean, another one, Noel?" Eve asked. "Did something arrive earlier for Alaina?"

"Yes —" Noel began, then noticed Laney staring at him and shaking her head slightly. "Ah...no, actually. A package did arrive, yes, it wasn't for Sis, though. It was addressed to the wrong house. It was for the Winston-Youngs, so I took it next door."

Eve nodded and finished her tea. "Aren't you going to open it, Alaina?"

"Now? Stephen's right, it's too early to open presents. I'll tuck it under the tree for tomorrow morning."

"Don't be silly, Alaina. Whoever sent it wants you to open it now."

Laney put down her knife and fork and slowly peeled the tape away. From the shape and size of the box she knew exactly what was inside and, as she raised the lid, she also knew what kind of a day she was in for. Underneath layers of gold tissue sat a brand-new pair of black velvet high heel shoes, decorated with tiny diamond clusters. In her size. And they matched the dress perfectly. The card simply read *'Guess who?'*

"Why, they're lovely, Alaina. Who would send you shoes? Seems a strange gift all on its own," Eve commented, reading the card.

Laney remained silent, determined not to tell her mother about the matching gown hanging in her closet. She placed the box under her chair and continued eating her pancakes.

"Heard from Mr. Hammond lately, Laney?" Stephen asked.

"No."

"No? I thought one of you would've at least told me about your lunch last week."

Eve's head lifted slightly, even though she continued to concentrate on buttering her toast.

"We didn't even eat. How's that for an exciting lunch?"

"Epic," Jamie grinned. "What did you do instead? Dance?"

Laney focused intently on the maple syrup oozing around her plate as she recalled her dance with Tyler at the DeSantis party. She was not delighted, however, that her brothers had remembered it, too.

"Mr. Hammond." Eve said. "Isn't he that charming man I met at our DeSantis party? The one who dances divinely?"

"That's him," Jamie confirmed.

"Do you see him on a regular basis, Alaina? Because that will come to an end once you're married."

"No, Mother. I told you before. He's an old friend, and he's always very busy. I rarely see him. We don't talk, we don't meet, we don't do anything."

Jamie smiled again. "Except dance."

"Jamie, shut up!" Laney tossed him a wicked glare.

"You said you met for lunch," Eve persisted.

"I happened to bump into him last week in Stephen's office. He invited me for a quick lunch, and that's exactly what it was. Quick."

"So why didn't you eat?"

"Too busy dancing, I'll bet."

"James, mind your manners, please. Tell me, Alaina, why would a man invite you to lunch, and not bother to eat?"

Laney took her time swallowing her last morsel of pancake. "We had ordered our lunch, then he got an urgent call on his cell and had to leave." She noticed Stephen was staring at her with a doubtful look on his face. Laney ignored it and finished her tea.

"I detest cell phones, especially at meals." Eve shook her head.

The lie seemed to placate her mother and Laney said a silent prayer for this inquisition to end.

"How do you know him, Stephen?"

"We've been involved in a few contracts, Mother. Nothing major, a few short-term deals."

"Is everyone ready for tonight?" Boyd barked from the head of the table. "It's a very important party, you know!"

The family chatted about the evening's festivities, Eve interrogating each of her sons to find out who they had chosen to bring as their date, and what colour gowns they would be wearing. Right, as if her brothers knew or cared about that, Laney smiled to herself. She noticed Stephen tried hard not to volunteer any information.

"What about you, Stephen?" Laney said with a mouthful of toast. "Who are you taking?"

"I, in my infinite wisdom, am going stag."

"Judith dumped you, you mean." Charles stated flatly.

"She didn't dump me, Chuck, we merely had an inexplicable inconsistency in our feelings for each other and both felt it best if we had a parting of the ways."

"It's Charles. And she dumped him."

"Charles, don't be disagreeable," his mother advised, as the main telephone rang.

"Laney, it's for you. It's Ramone." Noel came back to the table.

Laney was ready for the next round.

"Did you get the shoes?"

"Yes Ramone. I got the shoes."

"No excuses. I want to see you in that dress tonight."

"Well, I'd really like to, it is such a beautiful gown, too bad it's missing something." Laney held the phone at arm's length knowing what his response would be.

"Missing something?!" he bellowed. "That dress cost me...missing something? You ungrateful —"

"Jewels, Ramone. It has such a low neckline I'd look as pale as a ghost unless I had the perfect necklace and earrings to wear with it. You wouldn't want me to look pale, would you, Ramone?"

Laney ended the call convinced he would soon tire of playing this game. It was nearly noon Christmas Eve. Ramone hated shopping at the best of times, so he certainly would not go out in the midst of last minute shoppers to buy her jewellery. She figured his only option was to phone the store to see if they had something in stock they could send over. Laney hoped not.

She returned to her room to look at the gown. It was undeniably the finest gown she had ever seen. And the shoes matched perfectly. Figures.

Later that afternoon, as she was wrapping gifts in her room, Stephen popped his head round her door. "Hey Sis, got a minute?"

"Sure, come on in." She turned the volume down on the Christmas CD she was listening to.

"I heard an interesting bit of gossip, thought you'd like to know, so you can prepare yourself, in case it happens to be true."

Laney frowned. "What is it?"

"It's about Tyler."

She stared at her brother. "What about him?"

"He'll be attending the party tonight."

The colour drained from her face. "What? He can't be! He told us, didn't he, that he was going away for the holidays?"

Stephen shrugged. "I guess his plans changed. Anyway, you know how many people go to Monty's party. It's a Christmas Eve tradition. And Hammond has known Monty for years.

"Is he going alone?"

"How should I know?"

"You know everything else."

"Not that. By the way, Ramone's here. Says he has a special gift for you and wants you to open it now."

"Oh, perfect. Here we go again. Tell him I'll be down in a minute, will you?"

"Sure. See you later."

Laney pushed the unwrapped presents under her bed, cursing and swearing as she did. Perhaps she could feign a migraine and stay home alone tonight. That would be infinitely more pleasurable than seeing Tyler again, and battling with Ramone over this dress. Their last telephone conversation was two hours ago. There was no possible way, on Christmas Eve, he would've had time to find a parking spot, find the right jewellery, line-up to purchase it, have it wrapped, and arrive here within that time. Then a thought struck her. Perhaps her prayers had finally been answered and he was here to take back the ring and call off the engagement, wanting no more of her and her meddling mother. A Christmas miracle! She hoped karma believed in Christmas.

But she was kidding herself, that wouldn't happen — too much money at stake. He's playing games. He must've bought the gown and all the accessories at the same time and he's testing me to see how far I'll push this. Well, let's show him! She marched downstairs directly into the path of her mother.

"Ramone's in the drawing room, dear. He has a present for you. Didn't you bring his gift down?" she asked when she noticed Laney was empty handed.

"No, Mother. I can't wrap what I want to give him."

"Really, Alaina!" Eve marched off, disgusted.

Laney opened the door to the drawing room to find Ramone talking on his cell. He ended the call abruptly when he heard the door shut.

"Here, open this." He tossed her a small package, wrapped in gold foil.

Laney examined the wrapped box carefully and shook it gently.

"Stop shaking it and open the damn thing!"

"Ramone, what are you trying to prove with this little charade? I'll be wearing my white silk tonight, and nothing you say or do or buy will change that." Laney tore at the wrap and lifted the lid. She let out an unwilling gasp when she saw what was inside.

"Like it?" Ramone looked over her shoulder. "I thought you'd like the most expensive thing in the store." He lifted the glittering diamond necklace and held it up to the light. "Here, let me put it on."

Laney stood still as he placed it around her neck, noticing the matching earrings nestled in a corner of the box. She ran her fingers over the stones, knowing they would lie at the exact spot to complement the gown perfectly."

"It's beautiful. Thank you."

"Thank you? That's all I get?"

"Isn't that enough?"

"No." Ramone seized her shoulder, spun her around and began kissing her.

"Stop it!" she shrieked. Again, Laney was revolted. She struggled to be free of him, which forced him to clutch her even tighter. His hands roamed brazenly over her body until she finally wrestled free.

"What do you think you're doing? I'm *not* your play toy! I will not be treated like that, Ramone! Keep your filthy hands to yourself!"

Ramone laughed and tossed her another wrapped gift from the table, where, Laney noticed, sat a collection of brightly wrapped parcels.

"Here, in case you had any more excuses up your sleeve."

"What's this?"

"An evening bag to match the dress. The sales lady said you'd probably need it." He pointed to the other packages. "And this is French perfume, this one has something for your hair, and this one," he pointed to the largest one, "contains a cape that matches the dress." He strolled to the door. "Don't ever say I don't care for you, Laney."

"You *don't* care for me, Ramone. You could spend all the money in the world on me and scarcely give a flying fig about me. You don't know the meaning of the word care. All you're worried about is that I look beautiful in front of your snobbish friends, and getting your hands on the cheque my mother promised you. I hate you Ramone DeSantis. And I'm *not* wearing that dress, I don't care how many parcels you've brought!"

"What dress?" Eve stood at the door.

"Mother. What are you doing here?"

"I came to see what all the shouting was about." She walked into the room and immediately noticed all the packages on the table. "Who are all these for?"

"You're darling daughter, who doesn't want them."

"What's this, Alaina? Why won't you accept these gifts?"

"You don't know the circumstances, Mother. You don't understand."

"What are the circumstances?"

Ramone sat down and lit a cigarette. "I buy this woman a perfectly nice gown to wear tonight knowing that because she's getting fatter, none of her other dresses will fit her, and she tells me she can't wear it."

"A gown?"

"Then I buy her the matching shoes, and she's still not happy. So, I break the bank and buy her a diamond necklace and earrings, and would you believe it? She still won't wear the dress!"

Eve faced her daughter. "Is this true, Alaina?"

With total exasperation simmering under the surface, Laney nodded. "There's more to it than that, Mother. Why don't you let Ramone and I sort this out?"

"Is this the necklace?" She gently touched the sparkling stones settled around Laney's neck.

"Yes."

"Why, Ramone, it's lovely. You certainly have excellent taste."

"I picked your daughter, didn't I?" He smirked.

"Yes, you did. I'd like to see the dress, Alaina. Where is it?"

Laney had had enough. "Fine, Mother. *You* can wear the precious gown. Here, take the necklace, too." She impatiently unclasped it and dumped it into her mother's hand. "Take the shoes, the purse, the perfume, everything! Have a great time! I'm staying home tonight."

"Don't you show your temper with me, young lady. Now I want to see this gown. And if I like it, you will wear it tonight, and that's final."

"Since when does everyone else choose what *I'm* going to wear?"

"Since you became pregnant, Alaina, you have been unable to make one rational decision. Someone has to do that for you. Now, I want to see this gown."

Laney reluctantly followed her mother to her room, Ramone nudging her up every step. She pulled the dress from the wardrobe and placed it on the bed.

"Why Alaina, this is from Dorman's! It must of cost you a fortune, Ramone!"

"Why is everyone so concerned about the cost of things around here?" Laney asked, not expecting an answer.

"I'd love to see you in this gown, my darling." Ramone said softly. So softly, Laney was astonished it was actually him speaking.

"Don't start the scorned lover routine for my mother's sake, Ramone, it won't work," Laney recommended.

"I don't understand you, I do so want to please you." He smiled.

"Oh, please! Since when have you ever wanted to please *me*? All you want is a slice of the Calderone pie!"

"Enough!" Eve turned to face them both. "Now I've heard enough arguing! You two will be husband and wife in less than two months. You'd better learn how to get along. Ramone, thank you for your complete attention to my daughter, you are a very thoughtful man. Alaina, you will wear the dress to tonight's party. End of discussion."

Laney watched her mother leave the room, knowing to continue the fight was pointless. Ramone smirked as he sauntered to the door. "See you tonight. In that dress. Limo and me will be here at seven." He slammed the door behind him.

"That's what you think!" Laney yelled. "This isn't over yet!" She darted to her wardrobe and pulled out her white silk gown, the one she had intended to wear. She stepped in front of the full-length mirror as she slid the gown over her head. As she reached to close the zipper, her heart sank. The two sides would not meet.

"No!" she cried. "I couldn't have gained so much weight!"

She fumbled and fought with the zipper yet no amount of coaxing would nudge it. She stood crestfallen in front of the mirror, watching her tears fall onto the glistening white fabric bunched up around her waist. Why couldn't anything go right for her? Just once? Why couldn't something be totally wonderful and perfect?

A tiny voice in her head reminded her she had already had that totally wonderful and perfect time with Tyler, and it was over. Things would never be the same, and she must adjust and adapt to her new life.

Laney's stubborn streak then took over and she spent the next two hours becoming increasingly agitated as she tried on all her evening gowns, cursing each time she couldn't get them fastened. Not a one. They were all too tight.

She finally flopped on her bed, the sobs coming hard and fast as she at last acknowledged the reality that she had a baby growing inside her. Even though she knew she was pregnant, she had never allowed herself to stop and really think about precisely what it meant. She had tried to deny the truth, thinking by not catering to her pregnancy, she would love the baby less. She could blame it for spoiling what little chance she had to be happy. But that wasn't fair, and she knew now she just couldn't do it. She was carrying a new life! A life she helped create! How could she possibly blame an innocent child for ruining her life when she was the fool to blame for letting Ramone get too close?

Perhaps, she thought, this baby will be the best thing that ever happens to me. I'll be needed and loved. I'll be everything to this child. This tiny little baby growing inside me will be part of me forever, and I want to give it all the love I have.

Perhaps it'll be a girl, a beautiful daughter to share everything with, or a boy, because a son would be wonderful, too. She smiled thinking how her baby would be continually spoiled by its four uncles, its grandfather and maybe, just maybe, its grandmother.

This baby will be the love of my life and I have to do everything in my power to make sure the rest of this pregnancy goes smoothly. I want to give birth to a strong and healthy baby. My baby.

Laney sat up and wiped away the tears. "I want this baby." She moved her hand over her tummy. "I really do love you, my little one." She hugged her pillow and smiled, her earth-shattering revelation filling her with immense joy and happiness.

Then a thought hit her. What if, by a stroke of luck, the black velvet gown didn't fit, either? She could stay home and enjoy the evening with a huge bowl of popcorn and watch all her favourite Christmas movies. She didn't even want to go to this stupid party, especially if Tyler was going to be there. She'd attended Monty's Christmas Eve parties with her family every year since she was sixteen, so missing one year wouldn't be a crime. And having no dress to wear was the perfect excuse!

Laney looked at the beautiful gown again. She squirmed out of the dress she was wearing and stepped into it. She gently propelled it up over her thighs, then waist, then shoulders. She was again in awe at how gorgeous the dress was. There was no zipper to contend with on this gown, instead tiny, round, diamond-studded buttons ran from the plunging V-neckline to her lower back.

Laney reached for the first few buttons and met no resistance in fastening the ones over her hips. There seemed to be an infinite reserve of velvet in the folds of the skirt that expanded, allowing her to fasten the buttons with ease.

The moment of truth. Laney's hands moved to the buttons over her waist, her fingers searching for each tiny buttonhole. The fabric was not as plentiful here, yet, to her dismay, the buttons fastened effortlessly.

Then Laney caught her reflection in the mirror. She approached it warily, not believing what she saw. She looked radiant, magical, like a Disney princess come to life! Even with the dress not fully fastened and gaping at the neckline, with no makeup on and her hair a mess, she looked incredibly beautiful. She'd never looked like this in any other gown she'd ever worn.

She was ambivalent. She honestly didn't want to go to this party, especially because her mother and Ramone had ordered her to wear this dress, and God knows what Tyler would say to upset her, yet she felt so rejuvenated by her new-found love for her baby that she wanted to share with everyone her joy about her pregnancy, and her eagerness to begin this new chapter in her life.

She got closer to the mirror, with every step the dress swirled around her. Laney knew once she did her make-up and hair, and stepped into those new shoes, she would glow. The dress was perfect and she would wear it.

# Chapter 13

The Christmas Eve air was crisp and cold and a few snowflakes fell as Laney and Ramone climbed the hotel steps. The two doormen greeted them, pulling the enormous glass and brass doors open to allow them passage. The elegant lobby had been exquisitely decorated for the holiday season with blossoming poinsettias everywhere, fresh pine and cedar garland with festive ribbon had been draped around the ceiling. There were crystal vases of multi-coloured glass ornaments, and huge Christmas trees trimmed with twinkling lights. Carollers dressed in Olde English costumes strolled through the hotel serenading guests with traditional carols.

Laney wanted to enjoy the evening, to savour the wonderful things which always meant a lot to her at Christmastime, but thoughts of her impending marriage to Ramone hindered that happiness. She had yet to accept the fact that he would marry her despite the unusual condition she had put into their pre-nup, and it saddened her even more to acknowledge he never really did love her but was merely using her to bolster both his ego and his bank account. And her father didn't seem to be having any success changing her mother's mind, the wedding date was looming ever closer. Would she ever know what real, true love was? Maybe, she thought, I'll have to settle for the kind of love a mother and child share. It's finally time to accept this situation and try to take pleasure in the little things.

As they entered the grand ballroom, a throng of friends descended on them. Laney smiled and tried to make conversation, then finally managed to excuse herself. She wandered through the crowd looking for her brothers.

"Hello Ginger."

Laney turned to find Tyler inches away from her. Her mouth went dry, and she licked her lips while struggling for something to say. Her thoughts bounced back to their last encounter, their quarrel at the restaurant, and she watched Tyler's eyes darken as he took in her dress.

"You look sensational. New gown?"

Laney looked down, her hands nervously smoothing the velvet at her waist. "Um...yes, thanks."

She noticed beneath Tyler's watchful eyes and sexy grin, he had on the traditional black tuxedo, this time with a silver silk tie and vest which, in this light, was the exact colour of his eyes. He looked devastatingly handsome and she turned away, sensing a familiar heat surging through her veins.

"It's spectacular. How are you, Laney?"

"Fine. And you?" Lord, she thought, here we go again with the absurd question and answer session.

"Where's your fiancé?"

STRANDED in LOVE

She shrugged. "Somewhere." Her eyes scanned the ballroom. "Are you here alone?" The instant the words were out of her mouth, she knew it was the wrong thing to say.

Another smile creased his lips. "No, I'm not."

"Do I know her?" That didn't sound as casual as she'd hoped.

"You know *of* her." He was beside her now, placing his hand in the small of her back, propelling her onto the dance floor. "Let's dance."

She swiftly stepped aside, shaking her head. "No, Tyler. No dancing. Not tonight." She caught his irritated frown before turning to find Ramone, who grabbed her arm and pulled her in the opposite direction.

"Stay away from that clown tonight, you hear?"

Laney raised an eyebrow. "Don't tell me who I can and cannot talk to, Ramone. You don't own me."

"It's for your own good. You'd better listen to me."

"Or else?"

"You'll be sorry."

"Don't threaten me." She removed his hand from her arm. "I'd like a drink, please."

Ramone sauntered off to the bar. Laney suddenly decided she needed a trip to the ladies' room to restore her composure. Her reaction to seeing Tyler again, especially in that elegant tux, had unsettled her, even though she thought she had prepared herself for it.

The ladies' was full of activity with women adjusting their gowns, touching up their make-up and adding a final spritz to their hair. Laney managed to secure the last empty chair in front of the mirror that spanned the entire wall, and began to search in her new black velvet bag for her lipstick.

"How long have you been in love with my husband, Miss Calderone?"

Laney looked up to see the reflection of an attractive woman directly behind her, staring down at her.

"I beg your pardon?"

"I'm Tracy Hammond. You're Laney Calderone and you're in love with my husband."

Laney's stomach lurched as she stared at the woman behind her. Tracy's short, shiny black hair was combed forward, framing her round face and her emerald green cat-like eyes rivalled the sparkling green sequins on her skin-tight gown.

"You're...Tracy Hammond?" Laney stiffened.

"Yes, dear. How long have you been in love with my Tyler?"

"*Your* Tyler? What makes you think I'm —"

"Don't deny it, dear. I watched your reactions when you saw him. It's so painfully obvious."

"Don't call me dear, and *my* reactions are *my* business. So is my love life. Anyway, Tyler tells me you two are practically divorced."

"Not anymore," she sneered. "He invited me to this party tonight. I wouldn't call that practically divorced, would you?"

Laney kept silent. The lead balloon which had been gnawing in her gut the past few days began to expand again.

"You won't have him, you know. The divorce proceedings have been cancelled and I'm moving into his condo in the new year."

"Does Tyler know that?"

"Certainly. He's the one who suggested it." A wicked smile creased Tracy's face.

"How nice." Laney tensely applied her lipstick, losing the battle to remain calm.

"I mean what I say, Miss Calderone. Stay away from my husband."

Laney snapped her purse shut, spun around and stood up swiftly, knocking Tracy off balance. "Don't tell me what to do, Mrs. Hammond. And I would strongly recommend you get your facts straight before you confront a total stranger. You see, it's Tyler who's in love with *me!*"

All the other ladies in the room stopped what they were doing and stared.

Tracy smirked. "Okay, dear. Have it your way. I hear you'll be married soon anyway, giving your bastard child a name." She turned and headed for the door.

Laney was faster. She seized Tracy's arm and twisted her around. "You horrid bitch! No wonder Tyler left you, you wicked, spiteful excuse for a wife! Did he tell you, Tracy, that he had never experienced such passion and pleasure with a woman until he met me?"

Laney smiled happily as she watched Tracy's face tighten and drain of all colour.

"I really don't understand why you've bothered coming back for him," Laney continued, "Tyler told me you were the most insensitive, inconsiderate and, how did he put it, ah yes, most insufferable bitch he's ever known. And..."

VICTORIA GRANT

Laney's smile lit up the room, "did he tell you that this is *his* baby?"

The blow hit home. Tracy staggered to the nearest chair and fell in it. "You're lying."

Laney smiled sweetly. "Prove it."

"Tyler can't have children. We tried. It can't be his baby."

"I think when it comes to conceiving, *my dear,* the problem is with you. Surely you've figured out by now that nothing grows in ice!"

Laney snatched her purse off the counter and walked out, leaving all the women staring after her.

When she reached the ballroom, she heaved a massive sigh. Why had she said such a stupid thing? It was one thing for Tracy to embarrass her about the baby in front of so many strangers, but did she have to compound the problem by lying to her? She must find Tyler immediately and explain everything before Tracy got to him. She dashed around the ballroom, eyes everywhere trying to find him, when she came across Stephen.

"Laney, you look beautiful! Where's Ramone?"

"Stephen." She grasped his arm. "I need your help."

"Sure, anything wrong?"

"Have you seen Tyler? I need to speak with him right away."

"What's happened?"

"I need to find Tyler."

"I saw him last at the bar five minutes ago. He could still be there if he got chatting with someone."

"Thanks. If you see him, tell him I need to speak with him as soon as possible, will you?"

"Sure, Sis."

Laney made her way to the bar, then stopped in her tracks when she saw Tyler talking to Tracy. He had a peculiar expression on his face, and Laney didn't need to be psychic to know what they were discussing. She hurriedly found Ramone and pulled him away from his friends.

"We have to leave. Right now," she demanded.

"Dream on, woman. We've been here all of five minutes!"

"I'm not well and I'd like to leave."

"Go sit down, you'll be fine once they serve the food."

"Ramone. I want to go *home*!"

"Why, what have you done now?" he snapped.

Laney scowled. "What's that supposed to mean?"

"This happens every time we go out! What is it this time?"

"I don't believe this! We have to leave now!"

"Leaving so soon?"

They both turned to find Tyler and Tracy standing behind them. Laney's unmistakable gasp did not go unnoticed by Tracy and she smiled maliciously. They had probably heard most of her conversation with Ramone.

"Laney, Ramone, I don't believe you've met my wife, Tracy. Tracy, this is Miss Laney Calderone and her fiancé Ramone DeSantis."

Tracy tossed her head, sending the shimmering black tresses dancing. "We've met. Or at least the girl and I have. Ramone, is it? Ramone, how are you?" She held out her hand, which he kissed.

"Laney, you look stunning tonight." Tyler couldn't take his eyes off her.

"It's a pretty dress, dear. Too bad it's a smidge too tight." Tracy sneered and moved a step closer to her husband winding a possessive arm through his. Tyler didn't seem to notice, or if he did, he chose to ignore it.

Laney smiled. "Thank you, Tyler. You look very handsome, as always. Ramone, why don't you go and get everyone a glass of champagne?" She shooed him away with her hand.

"Does he always obey commands, just like a puppy dog?" Tracy asked innocently as Ramone headed to the bar.

Laney smiled sweetly, ignoring her remark. "Tyler, Stephen was looking for you earlier. He has some ideas he'd like to discuss with you. Shall we go and find him?"

"I saw him already, thanks, Laney. We're waiting until the new year before we start anything new."

Tracy continued to glare at Laney, contempt etched in her face.

"Is your mother here tonight?" Tyler asked, finally able to tear his eyes away from Laney. He looked around the huge ballroom. "We need to have a little chat with her, don't we, Laney?"

"We do?"

"Of course you do," Tracy snapped angrily. "You probably have a lot of explaining to do about your secret affair."

"Tracy, shut up." Tyler commanded and peeled her arm off his.

Laney smiled sweetly. "Does she always obey commands, just like a puppy dog, Tyler?"

"Ladies, ladies, let's not start anything tonight, all right? Let's have a nice time and leave the past in the past."

"A little hard to do, wouldn't you say, Tyler, with this girl carrying your child?" Tracy spat.

Laney's eyes widened as she watched Tyler's stunned expression change from bewilderment to...was that amusement? Clearly, Tracy had not told him about their conversation in the ladies' after all.

Tracy and Laney stared defiantly at each other waiting to see who would make the next move.

"Tracy, Laney, I've spotted Timothy Rochester and I must have a word with him. Can I leave you two alone? Do you promise to behave yourselves?"

"We're not children, Tyler dearest." Tracy chided. "At least I'm over twenty-one."

"More like forty-one, I'd say." Laney dug.

"Hell." Tyler sighed. "Tracy, go and get drunk. Laney, come with me."

Before either could object, Tyler grabbed Laney's arm and pulled her swiftly through the crowd. Tracy's sarcastic laughter echoed loudly behind them as Tyler kept moving. He led her briskly through the ballroom, into the lobby, and to a waiting, empty elevator that he guided her into and twirled her around to face him.

"What is going on with you two?"

"It's a long story," Laney said softly as Tyler pushed the button for the top floor.

"We appear to have lots of time."

"I'm sorry." Laney fidgeted nervously, lacing and unlacing her hands. "I didn't plan to lie to her about the baby, Tyler! But she was so nasty to me! I had to fight back!"

"You didn't have to, Laney."

"Yes, I did! You don't know what she said to me! Or how she said it! She's a cruel, heartless bitch and I can't believe you ever married her! And why would you bring her here tonight?"

"She dropped by to see me this morning. She needed my signature on some financial documents, and I asked her to come along tonight." He moved closer, his knuckles gently stroking her cheek. "Besides," he added in a whisper, "the lady I wanted to be with had other plans."

Their eyes locked, shock waves reverberating through Laney's body. "Let's not get into that again, Tyler. You know why I'm marrying Ramone."

Tyler leaned into her, his hands moving slowly and sensuously down her arms. "You don't know, do you, how truly beautiful you are?" he whispered, then lowered his mouth and kissed her with such passion her legs went weak, and she had to clutch the brass hand rail for support. His warm tongue darted in circles in her mouth, teasing and tempting her to follow along, as his hands moved to her lower back and bottom crushing the velvet deeper into his palms, pressing his body intimately against hers. Laney quivered at his touch, her body becoming compliant and moulding to his. She felt his arousal and tried to pull away, his familiar scent whirling around her.

"You can't run, Laney," he murmured, releasing his hold on her slightly, so he could place tiny kisses behind her ear, his hands circling her waist again.

Laney rested her head on his shoulder and closed her eyes. The strength had not returned to her legs and she leaned on Tyler while she tried to catch her breath.

This must stop, she told herself. I can't keep wanting to feel this way! But she knew it was the greatest feeling in the world. Her heart pounded wildly and she sensed the dampness between her legs and a hollow ache deep within her. Only Tyler could ignite this spark.

She sighed heavily and released herself from his hold. "I'm sorry I lied to Tracy, Tyler."

"Don't be," he said gently. "Believe me, my sweet, it's not worth getting upset over."

"I'll tell her the truth. I'll apologize to her."

"You'll do no such thing!" he informed her, holding and kissing her hands. "I rather enjoyed seeing her squirm."

"You're not angry with me?"

"No, just tell me first next time, okay?" he grinned.

The elevator doors opened and Tyler took Laney down the vacant hallway. They passed all the numbered rooms until they came to an unmarked door at the end of the hall. He pulled it open and gestured for her to go through. He followed her into a dark alcove, empty except for a staircase.

"Come on." He took her hand again and helped her climb the stairs.

She smiled. "Another rooftop? No snowball fights this time. We're not quite dressed for it."

"I can't be held accountable for anything I do on a rooftop."

At the top of the stairs was a huge, heavy door marked *Fire Exit*.

"Where's the fire?" Laney grinned.

"In my heart," he breathed into her ear, sending mega-watt jolts through every strand of her DNA.

"Won't the fire alarm go off if we open this door?" Laney asked, having a moment of clarity.

Tyler opened the door and Laney followed him onto the rooftop of the hotel. "No. It's there to warn people, it isn't hooked up to any alarm." He turned to her. "No one will find us here."

Laney shivered. "Oh, they'll find us. We'll be corpses, but they will find us!"

Tyler took off his tuxedo jacket, stepped behind her and wrapped it around her shoulders, then wound his arms around her waist. "It's magnificent, isn't it?" he whispered into her ear.

Laney's eyes roamed the skyline of the city where the neon street lights flickered, Christmas lights twinkled and a few flakes of snow fluttered to earth. She watched the cars and buses and streetcars down below, and the crowds of last minute Christmas shoppers rushing to get home to start their holiday celebrations, yet she could hear nothing except the pounding of her own heart. Laney put her head on Tyler's shoulder and felt his arms tighten around her.

"What are we doing up here?" she asked.

"I wanted to be alone with you."

"Why?"

"Because I didn't want anyone to see this." Tyler turned her in his arms. His hands cupped her face and he pressed his lips to hers. Laney dissolved into him, resisting all thoughts to the contrary that had surfaced not five minutes ago in the elevator. She could not control the heat that swept through her, compelling her to return his ardent kisses.

Finally, she pulled back. "Stop," she moaned softly. "Tyler, you must stop."

"Why? I don't want to stop, you don't want to stop."

Laney stepped away. "Let's go inside. It's too cold up here."

"Not yet. I want you all to myself for a while."

Tyler's cell phone rang and he swore under his breath when he saw the caller ID. "Tracy." He shut the device off without answering it and returned it to his pocket.

"Tell me something." Laney wandered around the rooftop, trying to put thoughts of his kisses out of her mind. "Why would you ever marry a woman like that?"

Tyler's eyebrows shot up. "You can ask me *that* when we both know the type of man *you're* going to marry?"

"This is not about him. I want to know what possessed you to marry that hateful woman."

"Let's not talk about her." He came up beside her. "Let's dance."

She smiled. "There's no music."

"We never needed music before." He took her into his arms again and they moved slowly on the frosty rooftop, two of them dancing in the snowy moonlight.

"Merry Christmas, Ginger."

"Merry Christmas, Fred."

Laney looked into his sparkling silver eyes, and the world stopped turning. The inexplicable charisma this man possessed captured control of her unstable senses again and she nuzzled into the warmth of his chest as they continued to dance. She felt his heart beating an erratic rhythm through his silk vest and when his hand gently pressed her head closer to his heart, she hugged him even tighter.

Then a sudden excruciating pain ripped through Laney's abdomen and she collapsed against him.

"God, what is it, Laney?" Tyler grasped her shoulders.

Laney, tears streaming down her cheeks, could not speak. She shook her head and clutched her stomach.

"Here, come over here." He manoeuvred her cautiously to an air conditioning unit, brushed the snow from it and helped her to sit down.

"Take deep breaths, Laney. You'll be fine in a few minutes."

Laney nodded, the spasms subsiding. "I'm okay," she mumbled, struggling against the tears.

"Is there anything I can do?"

"Hold me."

Tyler sat beside her and pulled her close." I'm calling an ambulance." He brought his cell out of his pocket.

She shook her head and rocked in his arms, the tears flowing like rain. "No. Please don't. I'll be fine in a minute."

Tyler rubbed her back and caressed her, hoping to calm and warm her. After a few minutes, he released her. "What is it, Laney? What brought all this on?"

She looked up at him, smiling. "It's you, Fred. You do strange things to me."

He chuckled. "It's nice to have a beautiful lady respond to me, just not like this. Are you going to be all right?"

She nodded, wiping away the last of her tears. "I think so. This isn't the first time this has happened, and I'm usually fine afterwards. I think we should go inside now, but..."

"But?"

"I'd rather not go back to the party. Could we go somewhere quiet and talk? You and I have a lot to talk about, Tyler."

His eyes held hers and he smiled. "Yes, we do. Here, take my hand."

He helped her to her feet and adjusted his jacket firmly around her shoulders. He lifted her carefully into his arms and carried her to the door.

"Why, Tyler," she smiled, "Aren't you chivalrous? This isn't necessary, I think I can manage one flight of stairs."

"Be quiet and open the door." He winked at her. "My hands are full."

Laney pulled the door open. Tyler carried her down the stairs and when they reached the bottom step, he softly brushed his lips against hers. "Are you sure you're all right?"

"I'll be fine. Thank you. For everything."

They reached the elevator as the doors were opening and a group of party revellers poured out. They whistled and cheered when they saw Laney in Tyler's arms and held the doors open for them.

"What about the others? We can't leave without telling them." Laney was curious what had gone on between Tracy and Ramone while they were on the roof.

"We don't owe anyone an explanation, Laney. Leave everything to me."

That sounded so right. So complete. She wanted to rely on his strength forever. "You can put me down now, Tyler."

Their eyes met, and she reached up to feel his lips again. Sensing her need, he lowered his mouth to fully take hers. Then, without warning, another searing spasm tore through her, seizing her body and taking her breath away.

"Oh Tyler, help me!" she sobbed, sweat beading on her forehead.

"Hold on, my love. I'm taking you to the hospital."

Tyler held her close as the elevator made it's way down to the main lobby. As he hurriedly stepped out, Laney's head on his shoulder, he saw Tracy standing there.

"What the —?" she began until she caught Tyler's fierce scowl.

"Hang on tight, sweetheart. We'll be there soon." Tyler moved effortlessly through the crowd, people parting when they saw him approaching. He passed through the ballroom doors where Stephen was chatting with an elderly gentleman.

"Stephen! Where's your car?" Tyler demanded.

Stephen rushed forward. "Tyler! Laney? What the hell's wrong?"

"God knows. I'm taking her to the hospital."

"Here." Stephen tossed him a set of keys. "It's the white Jag right out front."

"Thanks."

"Hang in there, Sis. I'll get the family and we'll meet you there."

Within minutes, Tyler was speeding through the city to the nearest hospital. Laney was doubled over in pain, sobbing.

"It's the baby, Tyler. Something's wrong with my baby!"

"Try to relax, my love. We're almost there."

Tyler swerved into the emergency area of the hospital and blasted the car horn. A few interns ran out to help Laney get out of the car.

"What's the problem?" one asked.

"She's in a hell of a lot of pain!" Tyler snapped. "Let's get her inside."

A nurse rushed out with a wheelchair and they carefully lowered Laney into it. Once inside, the nurse guided her towards the examination rooms.

"Wait..." Laney whispered.

"What is it?" the nurse asked.

"Tyler?"

"I'm here, sweetheart. You go with the nurse now." He kneeled down beside her.

"Will you stay?" she asked, her body soaked in perspiration, her eyes wide with fear.

His hand gently caressed her cheek. "I'm not going anywhere without you, Ginger. Now let them take care of you." He kissed her forehead softly, then watched as the nurse took her into the first room.

Tyler turned to one of the interns. "Be sure to tell the doctor she's pregnant."

The intern nodded and followed the nurse.

# Chapter 14

When she awoke, Laney found herself lying in a darkened hospital room with a dull pain in the pit of her stomach. Every muscle ached and she could barely move her head. She blinked a few times, her eyes trying to adjust to the dim light.

"Laney? Are you awake?"

She tried to smile when she heard that familiar voice. "Tyler."

"I'm right here." He took her hand and she turned her head slightly and found him sitting on the bed beside her, his usual impeccable grooming non-existent. His tie was undone and loosely draped around his neck, his hair was in complete disarray and weary dark circles had formed under his eyes. His vest was undone, as were the first few buttons of his shirt, and his sleeves were rolled up. His tuxedo jacket lay in a heap at the bottom of the bed.

She frowned. "What time is it?"

"It's very early Christmas morning." He smiled.

"What happened to me?"

"You're going to be fine, Laney." He squeezed her hand. "How do you feel?"

"Exhausted. My entire body aches. The last thing I remember, you and I were on the roof of the hotel."

"Yes. Kissing, if I recall." He winked.

She smiled. "I feel so weak."

"My kisses have a tendency to do that to you," he teased. "You'll feel this way for a while, my sweet, why don't you try to get some sleep now? I'll be right here if you need anything."

The door opened and Ramone barged through. "What the hell is going on in here, Hammond? What have you done to her?"

Tyler sprang up and stopped Ramone before he reached the bed. "Listen, you imbecile, if you want to discuss things, this is not the place to do it. Let's step out into the hall."

Ramone was ready to take him up on his offer when the door opened again. A doctor walked in and immediately noticed the tension between the two men. "If you two want to fight, do it in the local tavern, not here. My patient needs rest and quiet."

"Doctor?" Laney whispered.

"Yes. I'm Doctor Wilson. How are you feeling?"

"What happened to me, Doctor? Is my baby all right?"

The doctor pulled a chair up to the edge of the bed and sat down. Tyler stood behind him and Ramone paced around the room.

"Miss Calderone, your body tried to tell you something tonight." He took her hand. "It seems that you're not ready to cope with a baby right now. Your body is not strong enough." He squeezed her hand warmly. "I'm sorry, Miss Calderone, there's no easy way to tell you this. You've had a miscarriage. We were unable to help the baby; the damage had already been done by the time you got here. I think you've probably been experiencing difficulty with this pregnancy for some time, although what your own doctor advised you, I don't know.

"This is an upsetting thing to happen. Keep in mind that you're young and once you regain your physical strength and feel better emotionally, you shouldn't have any problems if you wish to get pregnant again."

Laney lay silent listening to the doctor ramble on that this was fairly common and how most women, if they took proper care of themselves, went on to have healthy full-term babies after a miscarriage. She didn't care. All she could think of was this baby. Her baby. The one she'd only just started loving and now she'd lost it. She'd lost her one chance at happiness.

"I understand there's been a great deal of stress in your life recently," the doctor continued, tossing a harsh glance at Tyler and Ramone. "I suggest you do whatever it takes to eliminate that stress before you try getting pregnant again." He stood up. "You rest now. I'll be back later to check on you." He gave Tyler and Ramone another warning glare. "Don't stay too long, she needs sleep." He closed the door behind him.

"Laney?" Tyler whispered. "Are you okay?"

"She's okay, Hammond! She'll be outta here by tomorrow. Now why don't you go find your wife and get the hell outta here?" Ramone dropped heavily onto the bed.

"Why don't you go and cash that Calderone cheque and get the hell out of Laney's life forever?" Tyler suggested.

"Why don't you *both* shut up!" Stephen came into the room unannounced. He kissed Laney's cheek and squeezed her hand. "The family's waiting outside, Sis. I wanted to come in first to be sure you're okay."

He turned to Ramone and Tyler. "I'm going to say something to the two of you right now and you'd better listen up. Both of you have put my sister through absolute hell these past few months. You both knew the delicate condition she was in, yet you continued to mistreat her. You," he pointed to Ramone, "have used her, abused her, loved her, discarded her and tormented her so much, I'm surprised she'll even speak to a man, any man, these days! In fact, I'm surprised you're even here. I see you went home for a change of clothes first, so Laney is obviously right up there on your priority list."

Ramone shrugged, shoved his hands into the pockets of his jeans and busied himself counting the ceiling tiles.

"And you, Tyler," Stephen continued, "have not been much help either! Throwing my sister into a whirlwind romance, harassing her constantly, then totally ignoring her because she inadvertently bruised your fragile ego. Not a big surprise that she's ended up in the hospital! Who can take that kind of torment and suffering in one relationship, never mind two? I've wanted to say this to you both for quite some time now, and I can finally say with all sincerity that I hope you'll both get the hell out of my sister's life forever!"

Tyler had been sitting beside Laney listening to Stephen's lecture. He stood. "You're right, Stephen." He held out his hand. "I've treated Laney dreadfully and I'd like to be the first to apologize. It will *never* happen again." He shook Stephen's hand, then turned to Laney. "Will you forgive me?"

*"I'd like to be the first to apologize!"* Ramone mimicked Tyler's words as he stepped in front of him. "Why don't you do us all a favour and go to hell!"

The muscles in Tyler's face tightened, his fist clenching at his side. He swore under his breath, then threw a punch so hard it spun Ramone around in circles.

"What the fuck?!" Ramone wiped the blood off his face.

"Get out," Tyler ordered. "And don't come back unless you'd like to lose more than a few teeth."

Stephen opened the door. "I think you'll find the emergency room down the hall and to your left."

Ramone stumbled out, flinching in pain. "You'll be hearing from my lawyer!" he yelled.

"Can't wait." Tyler turned to Laney. "Are you all right, Laney?"

Laney stared into space. "My baby..." she whispered, then the sobs began as the realization of last night's events hit her.

"Do you mind, Stephen?" Tyler asked. "I'd like to be alone with her. Can you stall the family for a while?"

"Is that all right with you, Sis?"

Laney nodded through her tears and Tyler raced to her side and pulled her into his arms. As Stephen quietly left, Laney clung tightly to Tyler, the sobs racking her entire body. Her fingers dug deep into his back and shoulders, her body trembling uncontrollably as she fought for breath.

Tyler rubbed her back and stroked her hair knowing his efforts wouldn't do much to ease her agony, yet he knew it was important for her to try to release the sorrow she felt. He rocked her for a long while, and when the tears finally eased off, he kissed her forehead, her eyelids, her cheeks, her lips.

"I'm so sorry, Laney."

Laney wiped away the few tears Tyler hadn't managed to kiss away. "Thank you," she whispered.

He frowned. "Thank you? For what?"

"Thank you for being here." She managed a tiny smile, then all the turbulent emotions rose to the surface again and another wave of tears engulfed her. Tyler drew her close, unwilling to let anyone else share this private moment.

"Let it all out, my sweet. I'm not going anywhere."

A long while later, Laney slowly tried to extricate herself from Tyler's protective embrace. "I'm sorry," she whispered. "I'm so sorry."

"Laney, sweetheart, don't apologize. You have nothing to be sorry for," he whispered into her hair, reluctant to let her completely out of his arms. "Everything's going to be fine."

She shook her head. "No," she murmured. "Everything won't be fine. I've lost my baby." She blinked back fresh tears. "I really wanted this baby, Tyler. I just wanted someone to love me."

"I'm sorry, Laney. I'm so sorry about the baby. I didn't realize how much you wanted a child." He dabbed at another tear on her cheek.

"Earlier today I finally realized that I was going to be a mommy and I knew I wanted this baby more than anything else in the world. And it's too late now."

Tyler turned away, swearing under his breath. Laney noticed his neck muscles tightening. "What? What's wrong?"

He swallowed hard and squeezed her hands so tightly she couldn't move her fingers. He looked into her eyes, sighing heavily. "Stephen's right. I've been a selfish, arrogant fool, Laney. I wouldn't blame you if you never forgave me for putting you through hell. My behaviour towards you in the past couple of months probably caused you to lose this baby and I'm so sorry. I feel responsible for this happening to you."

"No, Tyler. It's not your fault. It's mine," she sniffled. "At first, I didn't want this baby, so I didn't take care of myself. I waited too long before I saw the doctor and when I did see him I didn't tell him about all the pain I was experiencing. I don't deserve to have a baby!" She yanked her hands away from Tyler's grasp and pounded them furiously on the bed. "I don't deserve a baby!" she cried, "I don't deserve anything!"

Tyler harnessed her wrists, stopping the onslaught and pulled her back into his arms. "Stop it, Laney. Stop beating yourself up. It won't help. This has happened and now we have to accept it and try to move forward." He stroked her hair and she rested her head against his chest, another wave of tears hovering near the surface.

"And how do you suggest we move forward, Laney?" he whispered. "Where do we go from here?"

"I don't know and I don't care," she mumbled into his chest.

"I care."

"Well, you shouldn't."

"Well, I do."

"Why?"

"Because I'm in love with you."

She shifted away from his embrace and stared at him. "What?"

"I love you." His silvery eyes sparkled in the dark room.

"You love me?"

He chuckled softly. "Yes, Laney, I love you. I know I have a strange way of showing it, but it's true."

Laney closed her eyes. "Tyler, please don't say things you'll regret later. If you're saying this because of what's happened to me tonight, I understand, but you don't have to."

His hands clutched her shoulders. "I'm not saying it because of what's happened tonight, Laney. I've been in love with you for such a long time. I never found the right time to tell you."

Laney's lips quivered. "It's not the right time now, Tyler. I'm engaged to Ramone." She glanced at the diamond ring on her hand.

His eyes twinkled, a tiny smile dancing on his lips. He spoke softly. "Yes, and why are you engaged to Ramone, Laney?"

She frowned. "So my baby —" she stopped short, her eyes widening. "Tyler..." she murmured. "I've lost the baby. So...no baby, no Ramone. Right?"

Tyler smiled. "Right."

"Oh, Tyler, I love you so much!" She wrapped her arms around him and hugged him tightly.

"Laney? Did I hear you right?"

She pulled away and smiled, tucking her hair behind her ears. "Yes, Tyler. I love you so much. I never wanted to admit it to myself, especially with the baby and Ramone. I tried to deny my feelings for you, but I can't and won't any longer. I love you, Tyler Hammond."

He drew her close and kissed her feverishly, his hands moving possessively around her back. Laney wrapped her arms around his neck, never wanting to be held by any other man again. Although losing this baby was heart wrenching, she knew with Tyler beside her that she could get through it. She could get through anything.

"Let's go away, Laney," he whispered, withdrawing gently from her caress. "Somewhere warm where you can regain your strength. And then we'll come home and plan our wedding. If you'll marry me."

Laney stared at him, a cold, empty feeling creeping into the pit of her stomach. She jerked her hands out of his. "Marry you?" she asked between sniffles. "I don't understand."

Tyler smiled. "I love you, Laney. I want to spend the rest of my life with you. I want to marry you."

"That's not possible." She shook her head.

"What do you mean?" Tyler frowned. "Certainly it's possible."

Laney's eyes narrowed, her chest tightening. "Haven't you forgotten something?"

Tyler shook his head. "I don't think so. I've told you that I love you and asked you to marry me. What I want now is an answer to my proposal."

"You monster! How can you even think of such a thing! You're a cruel, heartless beast! Get out, Tyler, get out now and never come back!" she screamed, shaking her head wildly, her arms lashing out to pound his chest.

"Stop hitting me." Tyler tried not to raise his voice and once again seized Laney's hands to stop her attack. "What just happened here? What did I say? What did I do?"

"How can you be so cruel? I can't marry you, Tyler! It's against the law to have *two* wives!"

Tyler stared at her. "Two wives? Laney, what are you talking about? You know Tracy and I are getting divorced. I told you that when I first met you."

"Tracy told me your divorce proceedings were cancelled."

"*What?!*"

"She told me it was *your* idea. *You* wanted her to move into the condo with you."

"Tracy strikes again." Tyler shoved a hand through his hair. He lifted her head up gently and looked into the warm brown eyes that searched his soul. "Laney, my love, she lied to you. I can't blame you for not being able to tell. She's done it for so long, she's a pro at it." He held her trembling hand. "Our divorce is almost final, Laney, I swear." He grinned and pulled his cell phone out of his pocket. "Do you want to call my lawyer?"

Laney tried to hide her smile. "No. I believe you."

"I'm happy to hear that. So, let's do this right." He slid off the edge of the bed, got down on one knee and held her hand. "Alaina Calderone, will you marry me?"

"Tyler, get off the floor."

"Not until you answer. Will you marry me?"

"Yes, Tyler." she smiled. "I'd love to marry you."

He sat down beside her again and took her face into his hands, kissing her so deeply, so lovingly, Laney was again overcome by emotion and sobs caught in her throat.

"Are you going to be all right, my love?" he whispered, after once again calming her cascade of tears.

"I will be. It may take a while, but I will be."

"We have all the time in the world, Ginger. Now why don't you rest for a while and we'll make plans later." Tyler stood up and reached for his jacket.

Laney grabbed his arm. "No, don't go."

"You need your rest, my love. And if I don't leave soon the nurse will come in here and kick me out. Besides," he slid the tie from around his neck, rolled it up, and tucked it into his pocket, "I'm a mess. I could use a hot shower and a change of clothes. I'll be back soon, I promise."

"What about Tracy?"

"What about her?" Tyler scowled. "She's probably already left my place, and if she hasn't, she'll wish she had once I get through with her. Don't worry, my love, let's concentrate on getting you well again, shall we?" He leaned over and placed a long, lingering kiss on her soft lips.

"What's going on in here?" Eve's voice boomed from the doorway, as she and Boyd stepped into the room. "Mr. Hammond, isn't it?"

Tyler patted Laney's hand when he saw the anxiety on her face, winked, then turned to confront her mother. "Eve, Boyd, pleasure to see you both again. Laney's tired and weak, but she'll be fine."

"What were you doing with my daughter, Mr. Hammond?" Eve walked up to the bed.

"Kissing her."

She was stunned by the sheer honesty of his answer. "Yes...I thought so."

Laney looked up at her father, who was smiling at her.

"Eve," Tyler smiled, "we have a lot to discuss, but now's not the time. I'll be back to see Laney later today, perhaps we can all have a chat then. Laney needs to sleep right now."

"I have a few questions for you, Mr. Hammond."

"They'll have to wait. Laney must rest, doctor's orders."

Tyler's simple yet forceful statement made Eve hesitate. "Then, goodbye, Mr. Hammond." She glared at him.

Tyler stood his ground. He refused to leave, knowing he would be submitting Laney to her mother's inevitable tirade.

"Alaina, how are you feeling?" Eve asked, ignoring Tyler's careful watch. She held her daughters hand. "You had us all very worried."

"Don't scold her, Evey. She didn't do it on purpose." Boyd came closer to the bed. "I understand it's you we must thank for getting Alaina here so quickly, Mr. Hammond?" Boyd asked.

"There wasn't time to call an ambulance," Tyler nodded.

"We'll go now, Alaina, and let you rest. We'll be back later." Eve kissed her daughter on the cheek.

Her father leaned over the bed and kissed Laney's forehead. "Lousy way to spend Christmas day, I'd say, Pumpkin, but we'll make it up to you." He turned and shook Tyler's hand. "Thank you for helping my daughter."

"My pleasure."

Eve bellowed from the doorway. "Are you coming, Mr. Hammond?"

"In a moment." Tyler took Laney's hand as her parents left the room. "I love you, Ginger," he whispered. "Now get some rest. I'll be back before you know it." He kissed her cheek then headed for the door.

"Fred —"

Tyler turned.

"I love you too." Laney smiled.

"That's the best Christmas present I've ever had. Now go to sleep." He blew her a kiss and closed the door softly behind him.

Laney sank into the pillows. Finally, the indefinable tension that had lingered within her for months slowly began to recede into oblivion. She had lost the baby and that deeply saddened her. And, she realized, with Tyler unable to have children, she wouldn't be getting pregnant ever again. She wiped away another tear. It doesn't matter, she consoled herself. Tyler loves me and I love him. And when we're ready, we can adopt lots and lots of babies.

She glanced at the engagement ring sitting on her finger and swiftly yanked it off. No need to keep this on anymore! Ramone certainly would not even entertain thoughts of marriage to her now that he didn't have to and she felt exactly the same way. And that was perfect because she needed to be Mrs. Tyler Hammond more than she needed air to breathe. She truly did love Tyler, and finally saying the words out loud to him intensified her feelings for him. Those days spent with him were more than a fantasy, a fleeting illusion. They were real. His love was real. Her love was so real it made her ache for him and she was convinced her life would now be complete. Merry Christmas to you, too, karma!

# Chapter 15

Within twenty-four hours of Laney's miscarriage, Ramone had been thrilled to officially call off their engagement. Eve was not happy about the recent events in her daughter's life, but knew nothing could be done about them now. She cancelled all the plans for the wedding, and kept her part of her bargain with Ramone by giving him the promised six figure cheque on the condition that Laney's pregnancy and subsequent miscarriage not become public knowledge. The last Laney heard, Ramone had promptly packed his suitcase and headed for the Caribbean, and she was overjoyed that he was finally out of her life forever.

A few weeks into the new year, Tyler's divorce became final. Now there was nothing to keep Tyler and Laney apart and Eve knew that. Laney also knew her mother had a secret fondness for Tyler and so it came as no surprise to her that when they announced their engagement, Eve was the first to congratulate them. Her brothers each expressed their best wishes for the happy couple too, especially Stephen, who boasted to Laney that he knew this would happen from the very beginning. He shook Tyler's hand and whispered so no one else could hear, "Hurt her and I'll kill you."

Tyler nodded. "Understood."

Both Laney and Tyler wanted a very small wedding, and following a few exasperating and prolonged arguments with her mother, who had always dreamed of a grand church wedding for her only daughter, they got almost everything they wanted. Eve was permitted, after a heartfelt and emotional plea, to invite several prominent members of the community and a few politicians, as well as a journalist and photographer from the society pages of the city's largest newspaper. None of that mattered at all to Laney, who, on a sunny Spring-like day in March, experienced the happiest day in her life when she and Tyler exchanged their wedding vows in the chapel at Toronto City Hall.

Following a two-month honeymoon in Hawaii, Tyler and Laney settled into Tyler's condo. Boyd had wanted to buy them a new house for a wedding gift. They thanked him and refused it, wanting instead to re-capture the magical moments when they first met.

About a year later, Laney arrived home from work early, talking on her cell phone as she came through the door. She finished her conversation, flung the phone into the air and screamed.

Tyler dashed out of his study and stared at his wife. "Laney! Are you okay?"

Laney tossed her purse onto the sofa and ran to him, threw her arms around him and started kissing him. "I'm so glad you're home! Oh Tyler, my love! You've made me the happiest woman in the whole world!"

Tyler raised an eyebrow and smiled. "Really? Mind telling me how I accomplished this magnificent feat, in case I want to hear you scream again?"

Laney laughed. "Here, let's sit down." She took his hand and pulled him to the sofa. "No, no, I'm too excited to sit. Let's dance, Fred."

Tyler laughed at his wife's light-hearted mood. "What's going on, Ginger?"

She twirled in his arms. "I have a very special gift for you, Fred. For us."

"Tell me."

"Are you ready?" Laney did a few more twirls.

Tyler gathered her hands in his. "I've passed ready and I'll go crazy if you don't tell me. Now!"

Laney laughed. "Okay, okay." She looked into his eyes, a huge smile covering her face. "I'm pregnant!"

Tyler's jaw dropped. He stared at his wife.

"Isn't this the most wonderful news?" Laney twirled around the room alone, leaving Tyler stuck to the floor.

"Are you sure, sweetheart?" he asked softly.

"Yes, I'm sure! That was Dr. Wilson on the phone confirming what I already knew. We're going to have a baby!"

"Laney, my love, sit down. We should talk."

"Talk? About what?" Laney was still twirling around the room. "Fat! I'm going to get nice and fat! Won't that be great?"

Tyler took hold of Laney's hands again and sat her down on the sofa beside him. "Laney, are you absolutely positive, one hundred percent sure that you're pregnant? It could be something else, you know."

Laney stared at him. "Tyler, I'm late, I'm sick every morning, and I have a constant craving for jelly beans on spaghetti. I am pregnant. Are you not happy with this news, my love?"

He squeezed her hands, a smile barely perceptible on his lips. "I can't help remembering all the tests I endured when Tracy and I were trying to start a family. More than one specialist said the fault was with me, that I would never be able to father a child, and now here you are telling me you're pregnant."

Laney disappeared into their bedroom, then returned and handed him a letter. "Read this."

Laney watched her husband's face as he read the letter, his expression changing from confusion to anger to astonishment. "When did she send this?"

"A few weeks after we got home from our honeymoon. I guess her conscience was bothering her and she felt she had to set the record straight."

"That's a first for Tracy. Laney, why didn't you show this to me sooner?"

"I don't know," Laney shrugged. "I should have, I know. I guess I wanted to surprise you with happy news."

Tyler shook the paper in his hand. "I can't believe Tracy could be so scheming and manipulative! She actually paid doctors to lie to me! She did everything in her power to place the blame on me instead of on her where it belonged, and paid specialists to change test results! Those doctors should lose their licence to practice medicine!"

"You always said she was an excellent liar and always got what she wanted, whatever the price. Blaming you for the lack of children gave her a reason to end your marriage. I'm sorry she did this to you, Tyler." Laney took the letter and ripped it into tiny pieces.

"That explains why she was so angry with you at Monty's Christmas Eve party. When you lied to her and told her the baby was mine, she thought we'd discovered the truth." Tyler chuckled.

Laney nodded. "I didn't realize it then, but I hit the nail on the head when I told her she was the one with the problem."

"Why would Tracy bother with all this trickery?"

"Because she's a bitch and thrives on hurting others, especially you."

"She could've told me the truth. We were practically separated at the time, it wouldn't have made any difference in our relationship."

"Does that go for our relationship, too? Does this baby make a difference, Tyler?"

He stared at his wife. "Everything you do, everything you say, everything you think makes a difference to me, Laney. Do you remember all those things I said to you at the restaurant when I thought Ramone's baby was mine?"

Laney nodded.

"Good, because I meant it then, and every word is true now."

"Really?"

"Yes, really. I'm in love with you, Laney. And now that I know what genuine, committed, you-take-my-breath-away love really is, I ~~know I never~~ loved Tracy. Hell, ~~I barely~~ even liked her. You are my world, Mrs. Laney Hammond, and I will love you forever." He kissed her, slowly and lovingly and perfectly, then moved behind her and wrapped her in his arms and nuzzled her neck.

"When did you know you loved me?" she asked, rubbing her hands softly and seductively over his arms as he nibbled her ear. He'd told her before, practically every day, and she knew she'd never get tired of hearing it.

He placed tiny warm kisses along her neck. "I fell for you when I first saw you covered in snow and mad as hell that your car wouldn't start," he chuckled. "And definitely when you were so upset because you thought I'd died in the elevator. You were so relieved when I walked in here, I wanted to ask you to marry me right then and there. And when I saw you in your red sequin gown, still my favourite by the way, at that party at the mansion, I couldn't think straight and lost I don't know how many night's sleep! I knew you had my heart forever, though, during our conversation at the restaurant. Knowing you could've trapped me into marrying you when I thought the baby was mine. But you didn't. You were totally honest with me, even though your heart was breaking, and so was mine."

"I knew I was falling in love with you when we were on the rooftop. After the snowball fight."

"I remember." He continued kissing her.

"I kept thinking what it would be like to kiss you and hold you and share your life. I had to put all those thoughts out of my mind because of Ramone and the baby and…" She shook her head.

"We're together now, sweetheart. And we're going to share our lives loving each other. And now we have something even more wonderful to look forward to. A baby." His hands lowered to her stomach.

"Our baby," she whispered, her hands covered his.

"Our baby."

"Are you honestly happy with this news, Tyler?"

He turned her around to face him and kissed her deeply, proving to her his total commitment. "Overjoyed." He smiled. "What shall we do to celebrate?"

She raised an eyebrow and wound her arms tightly around his neck. "I can think of a few fun things." They shared another deep, intimate kiss.

He patted her bottom. "So can I, my love, but it's only two o'clock in the afternoon."

Laney took Tyler's hand and led him to the door. "How about a rooftop dance, Fred?"

"I'm right behind you, Ginger."